"Sweet L

gers sliding ***her hair. "I should run like hell, shouldn't I? But all I want to do is kiss you."***

"Yes," Elaina said. She was tired of running away.

"Yes, what?" His smile hovered just above her lips. "Yes, I should run, or yes, I should kiss you?"

Her hand lay flat on his chest, feeling the warmth of him through his shirt, feeling the soft, curling hairs beneath the cloth. She ached to touch it. Instead, she slipped her hands around his chest, under his arm, to his back.

His lips brushed hers again, not kissing, just asking again. He had never asked permission before. He was asking about more than a kiss.

She drew a deep breath. It was filled with his scent and made her dizzy. "I understand running, if you're not used to it, can cause heart attacks."

"That's true," he said solemnly. He brushed her lips again and she felt herself growing meltingly soft, felt her fingers cling to his back.

"Better not to take any unnecessary risks," she murmured, and he nodded just before he covered her lips with his own. . . .

WHAT ARE *LOVESWEPT* ROMANCES?

They are stories of true romance and touching emotion. We believe those two very important ingredients are constants in our highly sensual and very believable stories in the *LOVESWEPT* line. Our goal is to give you, the reader, stories of consistently high quality that may sometimes make you laugh, sometimes make you cry, but are always fresh and creative and contain many delightful surprises within their pages.

Most romance fans read an enormous number of books. Those they truly love, they keep. Others may be traded with friends and soon forgotten. We hope that each *LOVESWEPT* romance will be a treasure—a "keeper." We will always try to publish

LOVE STORIES YOU'LL NEVER FORGET
BY AUTHORS YOU'LL ALWAYS REMEMBER

The Editors

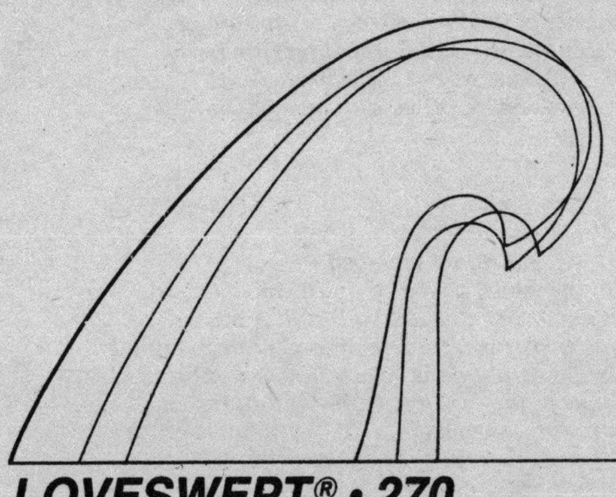

LOVESWEPT® • 270

Judy Gill

Pockets Full of Joy

BANTAM BOOKS
TORONTO • NEW YORK • LONDON • SYDNEY • AUCKLAND

POCKETS FULL OF JOY

A Bantam Book / August 1988

LOVESWEPT® and the wave device are registered trademarks of Bantam Books, a division of Bantam Doubleday Dell Publishing Group, Inc. Registered in U.S. Patent and Trademark Office and elsewhere.

If you would be interested in receiving protective vinyl covers for your Loveswept books, please write to this address for information:

Loveswept
Bantam Books
P.O. Box 985
Hicksville, NY 11802

ISBN 0-553-21920-0

Published simultaneously in the United States and Canada

Bantam Books are published by Bantam Books, a division of Bantam Doubleday Dell Publishing Group, Inc. Its trademark, consisting of the words "Bantam Books" and the portrayal of a rooster, is Registered in U.S. Patent and Trademark Office and in other countries. Marca Registrada. Bantam Books, 666 Fifth Avenue, New York, New York 10103.

PRINTED IN THE UNITED STATES OF AMERICA

O 0 9 8 7 6 5 4 3 2 1

One

The doorbell rang. The long, offensive peal of sound made Elaina McIvor jump and scrawl an unwanted line of red across the back of the zebra on her drawing board. Harrison arched his back and leaped soundlessly to the floor, then followed her as she slid from her stool and walked toward the door.

"Those kids," she muttered. "As flattering as all this is, I wish they'd get over their fascination with having me live next door." They were nice kids, she supposed, as far as kids went. Not that she knew a lot about children, in spite of the fact that they were the focus of her work. She knew even less about living in suburbia. But in the week she'd been here, her next door neighbors' two sons had disturbed her at work about twenty times a day. She was never going to get her current project completed at this rate, and then she'd be in trouble with the publisher who'd given her the job of illustrating the darned book. Oh, what the heck, she thought. Who'd ever heard of a red-and-white zebra in the first place?

The bell was ringing again, a loud, irritating buzz instead of the nice, melodious chimes she'd had in her apartment. Maybe, she mused, she'd read those two little boys the story and threaten them with the same fate as its characters. That should put some distance between their visits.

She snatched open the door, ready to address her junior-sized neighbors, but instead her eyes met a pair of brown, bony knees. A large, overstuffed pink-and-blue plastic tote bag was bumping against them, with a baby bottle sticking out of the top. Those knees were connected to a pair of deeply tanned, muscular thighs with curling dark hair covering them right up to the ragged edges of a pair of cutoffs, cutoffs that clung tightly to slim hips and a flat belly. An expanse of bare skin extended above the faded denim shorts, terminating where the hem of a half-length T-shirt covered it. An arrow of curling hair seemed to stitch the two garments together. A plump, pink baby was perched astride that narrow waist, wearing a yellow sunsuit and a happy grin. Elaina raised her startled gaze up and up and up until she encountered a pair of merry green eyes under dark brows. "Hi," said the owner of those eyes. "You Elaina McIvor?"

"Yes." She couldn't say anything else. The size of the man took her breath away. She was nearly six feet tall herself, and he towered over her. On his hip, the baby looked ridiculously tiny.

He smiled and said, "Oh, good. It's taken me hours to track you down. I'm Dr. Bradshaw."

At her blank look, he added, "From University Hospital? Margo Lawrence is my patient so I volunteered to bring the baby." He thrust the baby into her arms. "This is Betsy. She's wet."

That was a perfectly redundant piece of information, Elaina discovered as her arms went instinctively around the child. The man put the bag down at Elaina's feet and leaped off the porch, ignoring the three steps leading down to the walk.

"Wait!" she called out. "Hey! What is this?"

"A little girl," he said, slightly impatient. "Betsy. She's eleven months old. Oh! Didn't they call you yet?" He smacked his forehead with the heel of one hand. "And here! I almost forgot. You must think I'm nuts. This will explain things." He reached into the back pocket of his cutoffs and hauled out a folded envelope. Leaning over and stretching out an enormously long arm, he stuffed the envelope into the tote bag. Then he loped down the walk to the disreputable green van parked the wrong way at the curb.

"No! Wait!" Elaina called. "Come back here!"

He slammed the driver's door and shouted out the window as the van began to roll, "Later. I can't stop now. I'll be back."

Then the van was screeching away, lurching as it shot over to the right side of the street, leaving only a little cloud of blue smoke. When that was gone, she could almost have believed that the van and the green-eyed man had been figments of her imagination. Except for one thing. Twenty pounds of warm, wet baby were riding astride her hip.

"Well," she said faintly, "this is the weirdest thing that's ever happened to me!"

What was she supposed to do now? Call the police and charge the guy with child abandonment? Call the loony bin and have herself committed for believing that any of this was really happening? Or pretend that wasn't a man in a rusty van, but a stork? Some stork. He was almost gangly enough to be one, she thought before she shook her head. No. He had been tall, that was true, but not gangly. In fact, he had been extremely well built. She sighed, thinking about how well built he was. The baby patted her face with a warm, plump hand and said, "Mama?"

"No way! Not on your life!" said Elaina, alarmed. "I'm not your mama, sweetie." The baby had the bluest of blue eyes and a light golden fuzz on her head. Since she looked nothing like the dark-haired, green-eyed man who had shoved her into Elaina's arms, chances were he wasn't her parent either.

So who was? And who was her mama? The baby smiled at Elaina, several teeth, as tiny and as white as seed pearls, shining wetly in her mouth. Elaina smiled back. "That's something we're going to have to find out very soon, isn't it? Not only who your parents are, but where they are."

"Hey, look, Miss McIvor's got a baby!"

Elaina removed her fascinated gaze from the baby's delicate face and pinned it on the pair of grubby little boys who stood at the end of her walk, staring into the yard through the iron gate in the hedge.

"Can we come and play with your baby, Miss McIby?" asked the smaller one.

"Her name's Miss McIvor, Petey," the older boy said, "and you don't wanna play with her baby. It's a girl."

"Oh. How do you know?"

"Look at it. It's got ruffles on its bottom."

Petey looked and scowled. "Oh, yeah." The two boys vanished, obviously having something much better to do than play with a girl.

"What a way to achieve peace," Elaina muttered. "Import one girl-baby and the boys disappear like smoke."

She carried baby and tote bag inside, determined to read whatever kind of explanation the crazy doctor had stuffed into the tote. She stood the child on her feet in the middle of the living room. The girl's legs collapsed under her and she sat down on that wet, ruffled bottom and began to howl. Elaina stared at her, bewildered. Was there something wrong with her? Were her legs crippled? She had taken her own weight for an instant, then simply caved in. Or had she crumpled from sheer temper?

Harrison came to investigate the noise. The baby stopped making it. She reached for Harrison's tail, saying something that sounded like, "Lemme at him!" But maybe, Elaina decided, it was merely the expression on the baby's face that said it. At any rate, Harrison wasn't concerned. He rubbed his neck and shoulder against her fat thigh and the child dug her little starfish hands into his thick white fur.

Elaina lunged forward to prevent certain disaster, but to her amazement, Harrison was purring. She backed off, taking the moment of peace to seek out the note she hoped would explain things a lot more fully. Maybe it even contained instructions on the care and feeding of an eleven-month-old child.

She stared at the familiar bell symbol on the corner of the envelope. "Huh?" she said as she withdrew its contents. "A phone bill?"

It was made out to Dr. Brent Bradshaw, who had a post office box at the university, and was for the standard charges plus three long distance calls to the same number in Buffalo, one to a number in New Mexico, and another to a different number in Buffalo. And it provided absolutely no explanation whatsoever. Elaina read it through twice and checked the reverse side, only to learn that three of the Buffalo calls had been made during business hours when the rates were highest. That information, while interesting, made nothing clear at all, and she was starting through it again when a horrific crash sent her whirling around. The baby was no longer in the center of the living room floor, but was over by the far window, hands full of greenery, hair full of soil, eyes full of tears, and mouth wide open, hollering again.

"Oh, no!" Elaina ran across the room. "Oh, darling! What happened to you? Easy now. There . . . Oh, thank goodness, you aren't too badly hurt." She turned from the cactus to the baby. "Young lady, will you please stop that noise? And give me those. Oh, poor, poor Brahms. You tore off three of his fronds."

She set her wounded plant carefully back on his stand, then scooped up some of the loose soil from the carpet. She patted it around his roots and straightened the fronds as best she could. The torn ones would have to be rooted. Luckily, that wasn't difficult with Christmas cacti. Brahms bloomed a lovely shade of crimson and she would be happy to have several more of him around. But she preferred to do the cutting herself.

The bellowing stopped and Elaina looked down, blinking, feeling suddenly like the lowest, most miserable excuse for a human being ever allowed to live. She had just given precedence to a plant over a little child! She had left it to Harrison to comfort the baby! What use was she?

"Betsy?" she said experimentally, trying the name out. The little girl looked around and smiled that rather infectious smile again. And most forgivingly, Elaina thought. She crouched and lifted the wet and now muddy baby into her arms, gently brushing Harrison aside. "Oh, you poor little thing. I'm sorry, baby. Let's get you cleaned up, huh? We'll worry about the carpet and Brahms later."

Elaina put the plug in the tub and turned on the faucets, adjusting the water temperature. While the tub filled, she stripped the baby, enjoying the enthusiastic way in which Betsy accepted having her clothes removed. She squirmed and wriggled and kicked and giggled. "You really are a cheerful little thing, aren't you?" Elaina said. "I mean, don't babies cry for their mothers when they're left with strangers?" Far from crying, Betsy crowed with glee when she realized she was about to be bathed. And when Elaina sat her down in the water, she promptly sank.

"Oh, my gosh!" Elaina cried, grabbing at the baby frantically. She missed, grabbed again, and hung onto an incredibly slippery little body. Betsy sputtered and gasped and giggled, bobbing up and down in the much too deep water. She seemed unharmed, to say nothing of unconcerned. Elaina dried her face with the corner of a towel and pulled the plug, letting water run out and not stopping it until only a few inches remained in the bottom of the tub.

"We live and learn," she said, gently splashing water over Betsy's back. "I only hope you live through my learning. At least the dirt is all washed out of your hair, though that wasn't the way I had intended to go about it." She looked at the baby splashing happily in the shallow water, sucking on the washcloth. "You sure didn't mind getting dunked, did you? I suppose, if I had to have a baby dumped on me, I'm lucky it turned out to be such a good-natured one."

And Betsy was good-natured—until the time came to take her out of the tub.

She screamed. She kicked. She waved her arms, fists flailing, catching Elaina on the face and neck until she got smart and wrapped the child in a towel, arms, legs, wet, slick body and all, then held her close, rocking her.

It didn't help one bit. Pacing, almost running back and forth, Elaina weighed a hundred different possible solutions to the problem and rejected them one by one, up to and including simply putting the baby onto the floor and letting Harrison take over.

"What do you want?" she asked. "What can I do for you?"

Suddenly, she remembered the bottle. She pulled it from the tote bag, snapped off the lid, and shoved the nipple into the gaping mouth. Like magic, the noise stopped and Betsy reached up to pat Elaina's face, her tiny hand soft and warm from the bath, gentle and tender and immensely moving. Biting her lip, Elaina sat down on the sofa, one leg curled under her and resting against the arm of the couch as she cradled Betsy close.

"Hey, little girl," she said softly. "I don't know who you are or why you're here, but I think I could get to like you."

It was true, and the thought amazed her. When she had been younger, she had of course expected one day to have children. She had wanted them, but Kirk had not. At least not for a long time, he'd said. He didn't think they'd make good parents. She'd gone along with his belief. It was easier, she had learned early in her relationship with him, not to try to force her views on him. He'd held them in such contempt.

Elaina sighed. Maybe he'd been right. No instinct, not even common sense, had told her not to make the tub too full, had it?

When Betsy finally fell asleep, Elaina whispered, "Now what do I do with you?" The answer presented itself almost at once: Put a diaper on her. The towel and Elaina's lap were both soaked. The bag in the foyer contained a small selection of things Elaina presumed were baby necessities.

She pulled out the various contents, and smiled at one. A cloth book—a very familiar-looking cloth book.

With Betsy still sleeping against her shoulder. Elaina flopped open the limp, well-chewed book. Her smile deepened at the line that read *Illustrations by Elaina McIvor.* She had literally lost count of the number of children's books she had illustrated, but it still thrilled her to see those words, especially in a book that some child was enjoying.

With the baby changed and stuffed—not without difficulty—into a terry-cloth sleeper, Elaina stood looking down at her sleeping on her bed, still not quite sure she believed what was happening. Now that she had time to think, the worries came sweeping back.

What if the phone bill man had kidnaped Betsy? What if she was an unwitting accessory to a crime? What if he wasn't a doctor at all but was a patient—probably from the psycho ward—and had snatched Betsy? Things like that happened all the time. He could even have stolen the phone bill to give his story credence.

She had to call the police. She picked up the phone on her bedside table, then set it down again. It wasn't connected yet. Maybe tomorrow, the telephone company had said. And maybe not until next week.

The man hadn't looked like a criminal, had he? she asked herself. That was, if kidnappers had a certain kind of look.

If they did, his didn't qualify. Her mind had absorbed his appearance like a photographic plate, she now realized. In addition to being tall, he was broad in the shoulders, narrow in the waist and hips, and powerful in the legs. And good-looking. Not classically handsome as Kirk had been, but there was something about him that appealed to her on a very personal level. Which was odd, because since Kirk, she hadn't felt attracted to anyone. She hadn't wanted to. What had happened with Kirk had been too painful to risk a repeat of any kind. But still, she couldn't get Dr. Bradshaw's face out of her mind. Or the memory of his hard, tanned body. He was quite different from Kirk. Could that be what made him so attractive to her? She hoped he'd come back soon.

Oh, cut it out, Elaina, she told herself. Even if he was attractive to her, that didn't mean he was attract*ed*!

Why then couldn't she stop thinking about him, about his laughing green eyes? Along with that laughter there had been a deep intelligence in his eyes, as if he were examining everything around him, sorting the input through a sharp mind, and assessing what he saw. He looked like a man she would enjoy talking to. A man who would have a lot of interesting things to say. Did she really want to call the police on a man who had such intelligent eyes? No, she didn't. Not right away, at any rate. The best thing to do was wait a while. He had said he'd be back. And it wasn't as though she didn't know who he was. After all, she had his address and his telephone number, not to mention his telephone bill. Also, the baby was sleeping so soundly it would be a shame to disturb her by having police officers and social workers come storming in here just because she had reported Brent Bradshaw for abandoning Betsy when she wasn't at all sure that that was what he had done.

"Haven't they phoned you?" he had asked. That meant someone should have done so, likely would have done so, except her phone wasn't connected yet.

So someone had given Brent Bradshaw her name, but not her address. He'd said it had taken him hours to track her down. With her recent move, the address listed in the telephone book was wrong.

She stretched out on the bed beside Betsy, kicking her shoes off and wiggling her toes. She undid her hair and let it fall loose and comfortable as she cuddled the baby close so she wouldn't roll over in her sleep and fall off the bed. The warmth of that little body curled next to her, the sweet baby scent of Betsy, and the sound of the child's soft breathing, combined with Harrison's purring were soporific. Elaina drifted into a sleep as deep as the baby's, not even moving until the scream of her doorbell jarred her awake. Feeling disoriented, she wondered why the room was so dark. Betsy stirred, sat up, and beamed at Elaina.

"You stay put," she admonished the baby. "That's probably your doctor come to get you."

She snatched open the door in response to the third impatient screech of the bell and staggered back as something made of wooden bars fell in on her. She grabbed it and lowered it to the floor, then gaped at the man standing in the doorway. He had a folded mass of chrome and plastic under one arm, and looked as if the burden might pull him down any minute. "That's the crib," he said, nodding to the object she'd laid on the floor. He gave it a shove with one foot, moving it so he could step inside with his load and shut the door.

Elaina stared at him. His green eyes were no longer merry. His face was gray with fatigue. His mouth drooped and his shoulders hung wearily. He returned her stare somberly.

Suddenly, ridiculously, she wanted to cradle him close as she had done with Betsy. She wanted to rock him in her arms and tell him to go to sleep. He really, really needed to go to sleep, she thought. Shocked, almost frightened by the intensity of her feelings, she stepped back from him, lifting a hand as if to ward him off. He didn't try to come any closer, though, even when the words, "What's wrong?" were dragged from her by his look of utter desolation.

He gazed at her as if she could make things better, as if she were some kind of miracle worker and he was desperately in need of a bit of magic.

"I'm not sure she's going to make it," he whispered, shaking is head. He set down the object he was carrying, then strode back out the door. He didn't leap off the porch this time, but plodded down the three steps with fine precision, as if the placement of his feet required great care lest they be set wrong and trip him up. He was wearing gray slacks now, and a long-sleeved yellow shirt with a tie loose around his neck and the top two buttons undone.

In the light from the street lamp Elaina watched him slide open the door of the van and drag out a stroller with a plastic bag and a teddy bear in it.

He carried the stroller to the porch and gave it a shove so it rolled toward her. She stopped it with one foot and started to ask what was going on, but he was trudging away again. He leaned into the van, then backed out, dragging something with him. He swung it up and placed it flat on top of his head, arms supporting it on either side. It was a mattress, she realized. A crib mattress, and now she knew without asking exactly what was going on. Brent Bradshaw was moving Betsy in.

"Oh, no, you're not!"

"Huh?" He kept on coming, backing her right into the house. He leaned the mattress on the wall, then leaned himself on it, closing his eyes. She thought he might fall asleep standing there and grabbed his arm to give him a shake. His arm was as hard as steel, and too big for her to reach around even with her long, slender fingers. His skin was warm over the ropy muscles. Something twinged inside her, a deep elemental response that jolted her.

As if he had felt the same jolt, he opened his eyes. Looking down at her, he lifted his free hand and covered hers. For endless moments they stood there with sensations pulsing between them, her fingers sandwiched between his hand and his arm, her gaze locked with his. Silent, indecipherable messages darted from him to her and back again until she was dizzy with confusion unlike any she had ever experienced.

She sucked in a deep, steadying breath and managed to pull her gaze and hand away. "Come on," she said. "Get this stuff out of my house! You can't do this to me! There's been some crazy mistake. I don't know anything about—"

There was a dull thud from the direction of her bedroom, a moment's silence, then an outraged howl. The latter had the effect of snapping Brent Bradshaw out of his standing doze and stopping Elaina's flow of words. Both leaped toward the noise.

Elaina got there first. Betsy was sitting on the carpet near the bed, head back, mouth open, bellowing, and Harrison was making circles around her, his tail puffed straight out, his ears down, his back arched. He gave Elaina a golden glare as she approached the screaming baby and spat at her when she lifted the child and cuddled her close.

"Harrison!" she gasped. "What's got into you? It wasn't my fault she fell off the bed! I told her to stay put!"

She chose to ignore Dr. Bradshaw's sarcastic repetition of her words. " 'Told her to stay put'? An eleven-month-old kid and she 'told her to stay put'!"

To the baby, she crooned, "There, there. Don't cry. Let me see if you're hurt." She laid the baby on the bed and began running her hands over arms and legs.

"What are you doing?" Bradshaw asked.

"Checking for broken bones." Surely that was obvious, she thought, as well as being the obvious thing to do. The child had fallen, for heaven's sake. It was just as she'd suspected: He was an imposter. Any doctor would know about checking for broken bones!

"I see," he said. She wasn't sure he did. "What," he asked, "does a broken bone feel like?"

Some doctor! She had no idea, but was sure that if she felt one, some miracle would occur and she'd recognize it. "Like—like a broken bone, of course."

"What happens if you find one?" There was a definite thread of amusement running through his voice. Elaina was not accustomed to being laughed at. She stopped checking and glared at him, thinking quickly. "Call an ambulance."

Sure, Elaina. With no phone you call an ambulance. At least Bradshaw didn't know she didn't have a phone, she thought, taking some comfort from that.

For want of something better to do, she resumed checking Betsy's extremities. Betsy continued to yell. Elaina found nothing that might be a broken bone.

"All right, Betsy," she said briskly, speaking to the child as her mother would have spoken to her under the same circumstances. "That's enough. Get hold of yourself."

Behind her, she heard a distinct snicker and scowled over her shoulder at him. He was standing near the foot of her bed, taking up far more space than seemed his rightful share. This was a big room, with a big bed, but with him in the room the king-size bed didn't look all that big anymore. When he crowded right in beside her and sat down on the edge of the mattress, Betsy rolled toward him. So did Elaina. Swiftly, she caught herself before she swayed against his shoulder. He lifted Betsy high above his head and made a raspberry that shut off her bellows as magically as stuffing a bottle into her mouth had.

"Wait! Don't do that!" Elaina cried in alarm. "What if she has a spinal injury?"

"She doesn't," he said confidently. "And if she did, you'd have crippled her for life the way you scooped her up off the floor. Don't worry, babies bend easy. They don't, as a rule, break." He tucked Betsy in the crook of his arm and swung himself to his feet, carrying her with him. "Feelin' better, Bitsy-Bet?" He tucked his face into her neck and blew, making a weird noise that she found hilarious. At least while it was going on. As soon as he quit, she began to cry again, this time a shrill, plaintive sound that cut right into Elaina's heart.

"Oh, she *is* hurt! She's in terrible pain!" Elaina said, not far from tears herself.

"She's hungry," Bradshaw said with great authority. When Elaina didn't move, only covered her ears to try to block out the increasingly shrill screams, he lifted a brow. "I said, she's hungry. Warm up some food, why don't you? She's starving. Look at her. Every time she opens her mouth, she squirts. That's her salivary glands in action. Means she needs food, so feed her, woman."

Two

"Oh!" Elaina glared at him. *Feed her, "woman"?* "Do it yourself, Bradshaw! You seem to know so much about all this baby stuff, and you brought her here, so you feed her!"

"Okay," he said, grinning as he passed Betsy to her. "I'll do that. You change her." He wrinkled his nose. "She really needs it."

Elaina agreed. She also knew that she'd been suckered. Why, she wondered plaintively, when there's a man around, does the woman always get the dirty end of the stick—or the baby?

Still, she couldn't leave the child in this condition, so she manfully—womanfully?—changed her, and put her back into her terry-cloth pajamas. They'd be warm for her to travel in, and just as soon as she was fed, this kid was traveling!

Still, Elaina found herself coming very close to wishing it didn't have to be so as she lifted the now sweet-smelling baby back into her arms, feeling the snuggly warmth, the trust, with which Betsy nestled close. She grabbed a handful of Elaina's hair and tugged on it. This must be what it's like, Elaina decided, to have your heartstrings tugged on.

Nevertheless, she set Betsy on the floor where she couldn't fall and quickly redid her hair into its neat, secure bun. She felt more like herself as soon as it was done, and much more ready to face the man she could hear crashing around in her kitchen.

The chrome-and-plastic object had been transformed into a high chair. Bradshaw took Betsy from Elaina, slipped her down onto the seat, then shoved the plastic tray close to her. He fastened a belt around her middle, buckling it at the back. On a back burner of the stove stood a small pan with water and a jar of orangy-brown goop in it. Elaina looked at the jar and shuddered.

"What is that?"

"Beef and carrots."

"Uh—why don't I just make her a nice sandwich?"

Bradshaw grinned and lifted the small jar out of the water with a massive hand. He stirred the contents with a teaspoon, then tested a small amount of the stuff against his upper lip.

Betsy crowed and banged her fists on the tray of the high chair, clearly excited that the glop was about to be stuffed down her gullet. She opened her mouth wide. Bradshaw did the same. He shoved the spoon in. Betsy's lips closed around it and Bradshaw closed his mouth. The spoon came out clean and went back into the jar. Again, two mouths opened wide. Again two mouths closed, one around the spoon, the other over air. Elaina watched in utter fascination. This was something she had never seen before. Betsy opened her mouth. Bradshaw opened his. Betsy closed hers. He closed his. She swallowed, he licked his lips. Elaina broke up.

He glanced at her. "What's the joke?"

"You look so funny! Did you know that you open your mouth when you feed her?"

He turned a dull brick-red. "I do not!"

For the next several mouthfuls he didn't. Then he forgot. When Elaina laughed again, he glared at her. "You do it, then."

"Uh-uh. Not me, Bradshaw. She's not my baby."

"She's not mine, either," he said, apparently startled that Elaina might think she was. "And call me Brad."

"Not Brent?"

He lifted one dark brow. "Nobody calls me that. I didn't think anyone at the hospital even knew it. So they called, finally, did they? I'm sorry I had to leave Betsy and run the way I did, but I was late back on duty after it took me so long to find you."

"What do you do at the hospital?" She was still only half convinced of his sanity—and his veracity.

"I work in the emergency room. I'm senior resident." He cranked open the lid of another jar of baby food, stuck the spoon into it, and again tested the food. No, Elaina amended. Not testing, devouring. And a second bite too. "You forgot to heat that," she said.

"Nah. This doesn't need heating."

"Then why did you test it?"

"I didn't. I tasted it. I like strained peaches."

She gave him a reproachful look. "You'd swipe the baby's food?"

"She can afford to give me a bite or two. Look at her. What a chub. I think one of the reasons her mother's so sick now is that she's done without almost everything so that Betsy could have what she needed."

As long as he was talking, he didn't open his mouth each time the baby did. He wasn't nearly as funny to watch, but Elaina began to hope that if she asked the right questions, she just might figure out what was going on here.

"What's wrong with her mother?"

Betsy shoved the spoon away, apparently full, and turned her head to avoid the next offering. It smeared across her cheek and into her ear. Bradshaw shook the spoonful back into the jar and used the spoon to scrape the food off the baby's face. He put that back into the jar too. Elaina shuddered again.

"We don't know," he finally answered. "She collapsed today on the street and was brought to us. They brought Betsy, too, of course." He licked the spoon. "Poor kid. She was more worried about her baby than about herself. She kept begging us to find you so you could look after Betsy."

"You really are a doctor?"

He sighed. "That's what the diploma on my wall tells me," he said glumly. "But I wonder."

"Why?"

He gave her a bleak look. "People die, you know."

He let the spoon fall to the tray and Betsy picked it up. She banged industriously on the plastic for a moment before flinging it away. It landed with a clatter on the floor.

Elaina picked it up and rinsed it off, then gave it back to the baby. She didn't want to look at the man with the pale face and the eyes full of misery. But she couldn't let his statement go unacknowledged forever. Finally, she nodded, touched his hand, and said, "That must be hard to deal with."

He turned his hand over and clasped hers. As he met her gaze, that strange, electric sensation again crossed from his body to hers, looped around and circled back, linking them by far more than tightening fingers.

"It is hard to deal with," he said. "I know I'm supposed to be strong and detached and hold myself aloof from my patients' pain, but I can't. Maybe I came into the game too late in life."

"How's that?"

Elaina's voice was soft, Brad wanted to curl up in it and warm himself. How could a person put so much caring into two small words? he wondered. And when was the last time he had felt so . . . so . . . cared about? It shook him badly to realize how much he liked the feeling.

"I was a medic in the army," he said, and was amazed that it was the most natural thing in the world for him to be telling her this. "I saw how much more doctors could accomplish than I could, and got out so I could go to medical school. But I'm nearly thirty-five and most of the other residents are in their twenties. They seem to be more resilient than I. I sometimes think I should have stayed in the army. At least there I didn't have to deal with little kids and sick mothers frantic with worry over what was going to happen to their children."

"Maybe so," Elaina said quietly, her serene gaze on his face. "But at least now you're in a position to help."

"Am I?" He looked down at their linked hands as if wondering how they had come to be that way. She tightened her fingers a fraction and he smoothed his thumb over her knuckles. Her skin was so soft, he mused, as soft as her voice. As soft as her eyes.

"Tell me about Betsy's mother," she urged.

He looked up again. "She's so sick. And so tough. She held on until she was sure I had got Betsy to you, and that you understood. Now she's unconscious. Almost comatose. And we can't find out why. All we know is she has a raging infection that's involved her entire system. So we've got her in isolation and we're pumping antibiotics into her, but I still have an awful feeling that we aren't going to be able to do enough."

His voice cracked and he dropped her hand. He walked over to the sink, facing away from her. "Hell," he said in disgust. "I'm sorry. I'm just a bit tired."

"And hungry," she suggested, remembering how he had eaten that god-awful pink pap with such relish.

He shook his head. "I'm too tired to be hungry. I'll help you set up Betsy's crib and then I'd better go."

She stood irresolute, chewing on her lower lip, staring at his broad back, at the yellow shirt stretched tautly over strong shoulders. Strong, but drooping. She looked at the baby in the high chair. Betsy was drooping too. Obviously, her nap hadn't been enough. She needed a good night's sleep. She'd probably only woken up because a bottle of milk wasn't enough food to keep her going all night.

How could she kick out an innocent baby whose mother was sick, maybe dying? How could she make things harder for this tired doctor? But on the other hand, how could she let her own life be interfered with in this way? The fact was, she couldn't. She had a deadline to meet and was having enough difficulty with the project. She did not need something like this. She just couldn't do it.

"Listen," she said, and he turned around. She wished he hadn't. It was harder to say this to his face. "I really do wish I could help, but truly, I can't. I don't know anything about babies. I'm not competent to look after one. She was eating dirt five minutes after you left her here. Then I filled the tub too full and she sank. And I let her fall off the bed." She remembered how she had checked for broken bones and felt like a fool. What must he have thought of her? He had to have been laughing inside the whole time. A doctor, for heaven's sake! Why hadn't he said so? Why had he let her go on making an idiot of herself?

"Kids eat dirt and fall off things every day and survive," he said, smothering a yawn with the back of a hand. "And you're the one her mother nominated."

"But you don't seem to understand. I don't know her mother. I've never heard of her. There must be another Elaina McIvor in the city. You've found the wrong one, is all. Let's look in the phone book. I'm sure the other one, whoever she is, will be glad to take Betsy."

He shook his head and let himself sink onto a chair. He rested his elbows on the table and his face in his palms, rubbing his cheeks. The raspy sound of skin over beard was one she hadn't heard for a long time. Her body's reaction to it startled her so that she only half heard his words.

"You're the one. The only one. Eugene isn't all that big a city. And you illustrate kids' books, don't you?"

That caught her attention. "Yes, but . . ." She drew in an exasperated breath. Really, the man was going to fall asleep right here. One of his arms had just collapsed and his head had nearly struck the table before he caught himself.

"Darn it, you wake up, Bradshaw! And pay attention! Being an illustrator of children's books does not mean I'm any good with kids. Or want to be. I've never had anything to do with them."

"Don't frown like that. It makes you look like Miss Harris, my fourth-grade teacher who used to pull my ear." He wrinkled his nose. "And why have you got your hair like that? You look a helluva lot more human with it down, Lainie."

"My name," she said crisply, "is Elaina." Nobody called her Lainie. What a dumb name. And her hair was none of his business!

He yawned again. "Sorry, E-lain-a," he drawled. "Where do you want the crib?"

She followed him out into the foyer. "Back in your van," she said, but he ignored her and hauled it into the spare room next to her bedroom.

"Look, you can't do this!" she protested. "I told

you. There is a big mistake being made here. I can't be the one Mrs. Lawrence chose to baby-sit Betsy."

He gave the sections of bars and boards a shake or two and it resolved itself into a loosely constructed rectangle. He inserted the bottom, which looked like the pegboard she hung her gardening tools on. With a few deft motions, he affixed the bottom and the rectangle took on a greater sturdiness.

"Bradshaw!" she called after him as he strode from the room. He paid her no attention, only came back with that stupid little mattress on top of his stupid head once more. That was it, she thought. He was stupid. He wasn't a doctor at all. He was an escapee from a mental hospital who had swiped a baby somewhere and was doing this because he didn't know any better. She felt almost relieved by the notion. That this entire event had no basis in sanity or reality was easier to accept than the alternative.

"There's a crib sheet in the bag in the stroller," he said, not sounding as stupid as she would have liked him to sound. "And a blanket too. If you bring them, I'll make up Betsy's bed. After she's had another bottle she'll probably sleep right through the night. She'll want a bowl of cereal for breakfast, the rest of the peaches, and another bottle. If you don't have milk in the house, I'll bring you some before I go back to the hospital."

"Bradshaw!" This time, it was a wail of despair. What was it going to take to get through to this man? Why couldn't he understand plain English?

"I know, I know," he said kindly. He continued

speaking over his shoulder as he went to fetch the stroller and its contents. "You don't want any part of this. You don't know Betsy's mother and you don't want to know Betsy." He nearly ran over her toes with the stroller as he shoved it past her. He pulled the crib sheet out of the bag, shook it out, and began stretching it over the mattress.

"But as she said in her note," he went on, "Margo feels she knows you, and—"

"But I didn't get a note from her!" Elaina shouted. "All I got was your dumb phone bill, Bradshaw!"

He straightened, hands massaging the small of his back. "What do you mean, my phone bill?"

"I'll show you!" she snapped. Whirling, she nearly tripped over Harrison who had come to investigate her raised voice.

"There!" she said in triumph a moment later, waving the envelope in front of his nose. "See? And who do you know in Buffalo that you called three times during the most expensive hours?"

"My mother." He blinked bleerily at the bill and nodded. "Yup. That's my phone bill, all right. I wonder where Margo's note is then."

"Me, too," Elaina said emphatically, then spun around as a clattering sound came from the kitchen. She beat one very tired doctor by only half a pace and came to a halt in the doorway to stare at a grinning baby. Betsy was sucking on the corner of a lace tablecloth while a sugar bowl, its lid, and a crystal vase lay on the parquet floor in small, glittering pieces. Sugar and pink roses and water were splashed everywhere.

"Oh, Betsy," Brad moaned. "How are we going

to convince Lainie that you're a nice little kid if you keep screwing up like this? I saw the pile of dirt in the living room. You upset a plant, didn't you? And then you scared poor Lainie half to death by falling off the bed." He undid the belt that held her in the chair, picked her up, and kissed her nearly bald pate. "You just gotta be good, sweetheart."

She gurgled and buried her fists in his hair. She shook his head with all her might, then tugged at one of his ears.

Elaina uncurled those tight little fingers. "Don't, honey-bun. He'll think you're Miss Harris." She was appalled that Brent Bradshaw might believe she was refusing Betsy house space because she was naughty. Babies her age weren't. Elaina didn't know how she knew that, but some instinct told her it was true. There could be no malice with such sweet innocence, she thought as Betsy launched herself from Brad's arms to hers, patted her face, and said happily, "Mama."

"Cute," Bradshaw said, grinning at the fatuous look on Elaina's face. "It's the only word she knows. She called the head nurse Mama too."

Elaina glared at him. "The note. Where do you suppose the note is, Bradshaw? Or is there such a thing?"

"There is, there is, I promise you. I . . ." He frowned. "I stuck it behind the visor. That's where I stick all my mail. I must have hauled out the wrong envelope this afternoon. I'll go look."

Betsy was making sleepy sounds and rubbing her eyes. She needed more sleep, Elaina thought, and remembered Bradshaw's words. She also needed another bottle. Elaina got milk from the refrigerator, realizing quickly that it was too cold. Even she, who knew nothing about babies, knew that. She poured the milk into a small pan and turned on the burner, jiggling Betsy who objected loudly to having to wait. She got an empty bottle from the bag Bradshaw had brought earlier. When the side of the pan began to feel warm, she stirred the milk, poured it into the bottle, and held it out toward the child. Betsy was ecstatic.

"Baby, it doesn't take a whole lot to please you, does it?" Elaina murmured. She curled up as before on the couch, cradling the nursing child close. She heard the door open and close, heard heavy steps coming toward her, then Brent Bradshaw filled the doorway. She was struck again by his size, his looks, and that indefinable something that stirred her in a way she wasn't used to being stirred.

"Got it," he said, crouching in front of her and gazing at Betsy as she sucked on the bottle. He curled a finger and stroked the baby's face tenderly. To Elaina's horror a very definite shiver ran through her, a shiver of a kind she hadn't felt for a long time. It was almost as if that finger had caressed her.

"I'll read it when she's finished," she said breathlessly, wishing he'd move away from her. "I'd rather not disturb her. If she's asleep, you can just lay her on the seat of your van when you leave."

He looked at her bleakly and walked from the room. A moment later she heard the sounds of him cleaning up the broken glass and spilled sugar in the kitchen. He returned, strode to the corner where Brahms had fallen, and stared down at the pile of dark soil on the pale fawn carpet. Harrison sauntered over, rubbed against his ankle, and was rewarded by a scratch on the back of the head.

Brad looked at Elaina. "If you'll tell me where the vacuum is, I'll clean up this mess for you."

She shook her head. "No, thank you. Betsy's asleep now. Will you take her?"

Silently, he pleaded with her. Just as silently, she resisted. Green eyes meshed with gray. Her heart argued with her common sense and she was dismayed at how easily emotions could win out over mind. She sighed. "Take her to her crib."

Then, lest he think her too soft, too eager to give in, she went on. "It's late. I'll keep her for the night. But just for the night."

His smile didn't quite put the merry light back into his eyes, but it did ease some of the lines in his face. He crouched again and slid his arms under the sleeping baby, then stood up with her. "That's good enough for now," he said softly. "Thanks, Lainie."

"Elaina," she said, just as softly, but with a steely note. She might be stuck with doing as he wanted for the time being, but that didn't mean he could call her anything he pleased. That was a silly, frivolous little-girl name, and she had seldom been silly and frivolous—even as a little girl.

He nodded and said mockingly, "E-lain-a."

As he turned, the note fluttered to the floor and she bent to pick it up. Unfolding it, she read the weak, feathery scrawl.

Dear Miss McIvor,
You don't know me but I feel I know you. You always draw such happy children and your animals are so sweet. I took Betsy to the library to see you when you were reading to kids there and I loved your soft, kind voice and your pretty eyes. Please help me. I'm sick and I don't know anybody in Eugene but my landlady who is mean and the people I work for who are all rich and busy and wouldn't care about Betsy. They said I have to give them a name of somebody here so I lied and said I know you. Please take Betsy till I get better. I'm so scared they'll send her to strangers. . . .

If there was a signature, it was illegible, and Elaina thought it was simply that the pen had fallen away across the bottom of the paper. She had only read at the library on two or three Saturday mornings recently to help out, and was sure she didn't remember Betsy—or her mother. But Margo remembered her. In spite of herself, Elaina was touched. Poor Margo.

Sighing, she refolded the note and set it carefully on the mantel. After setting a candlestick on top of it for safety, she walked into the spare room to speak to Brent Bradshaw, who had tactfully left her alone to read the note.

Tactfully? She nearly hooted the word aloud. The man wasn't being tactful at all. He had simply fallen asleep on the single bed.

"Bradshaw?" she said. He didn't move.

She shook him. He grumbled and rolled over,

putting both shoes on the spread. With an impatient snatch of breath, she tugged his shoes off and set them neatly on the floor under the edge of the bed. Then, resignedly, she pulled a warm quilt from the top shelf of the closet and covered him, turned off the light, and closed the door halfway.

What with her unexpected afternoon nap, as well as everything she had on her mind, it was a long time before Elaina got to sleep. It seemed she had just done so when the oddest noise awakened her. It was as insistent as her doorbell if not quite as strident, and she had no idea where it was coming from.

She got out of bed, blinking blearily, and rolled up the blind. It was barely dawn. What could be making a noise like that at this time of morning?

She staggered out as the door to the spare room opened and a huge, shaggy figure stumbled into the hall, mumbling incomprehensibly. He blundered toward her as she shoved her hair out of her eyes, trying to figure things out. Nothing became clearer, especially when he walked right into her. His arms swung around her as she lost her balance, teetering on one foot. She clung to him with both arms around his middle, eyes squeezed tightly closed.

Three

It was the most incredible thing, Elaina thought with the few of her scattered wits she could gather. For the first time in her life she fit exactly right against a man. As the strange noise continued, she pressed herself even closer, noticing that her forehead rested exactly where it should into the curve of his shoulder, that her arms, snugged around his waist, didn't need to reach either too far up or too far down. She noticed, too, that her heart was slamming against her ribs and that she wasn't breathing at all regularly. Dimly, she realized she should move away from him, but his arms held her so securely she wasn't sure she could. Besides, she didn't want to. What she wanted to do was keep on leaning against his big, hard, warm body and go back to sleep. Oh, this felt great! Not only had her head found a comfy home on his shoulder, not only was she breathing in a scent that was unique and tantalizing, not only did her arms go around him at just the right height, but her thighs meshed with his and her hips nestled against a burgeoning hardness that was doing even stranger things to her body and—

What in heaven's name was she doing?

"Let me go!" she gasped, tearing herself away from him.

"Hey, who was hanging onto whom?"

"I . . ." Lord, but this man had bad manners! What a thing to ask. Even if it were true. He wasn't a gentleman or he wouldn't have mentioned it. But at least he had let her go. Had it been reluctantly? Her heart did dumb things again, thinking that yes, it had been reluctantly. "What's that noise?" she demanded, stepping well clear of him.

"Oh. Yeah." He looked guilty as he fumbled at his waist and the noise ceased. "My beeper. Where's the phone?"

She explained that it wasn't connected and unlocked the door to let him out.

He mumbled something, headed for the steps, missed them entirely, and fell off the porch, full length onto the grass. Shaking his head, he got up and headed for his van. She wondered if he were suffering from the same weird effects as she, if he couldn't walk straight because of that inadvertent embrace, or simply hadn't woken up yet.

He managed to start the engine and turn on the headlights of his van, so presumably he was beginning to function properly. She stood shivering in the dawn air for a long moment, wondering if and when *she* would function properly again.

Back in her bedroom she caught sight of herself

in the mirror, and stared. Her eyes were enormous. Her lips were parted as if waiting to be kissed. Were they? Probably. Damn! What had he done to her? She blinked. He had made her look . . . pretty, that was what he had done to her. And she was plain. But no, she reminded herself, "plain" had been Kirk's assessment of her. She didn't have to go along with it. She had told herself a long time ago that his opinion wasn't necessarily valid. In the past three years, she'd had a few dates. Not many, but enough to let her know that not all men found her unattractive. And Kirk had been excusing himself. If he'd taken up with a good-looking woman, his actions might have been less forgivable, or something. She'd spent a good many hours trying to figure it, and him, out.

She tried to remember if Kirk had ever said in so many words that he thought she was plain, but decided it must only have been his attitude. "You really should wear darker colors, Elaina. Why draw attention to your size?" For a long time, she had felt like an elephant. To hear Kirk talk, you'd have thought she was overweight, instead of five feet ten and slender. Models were built like her, except she was more busty than most.

The trouble was, she'd been so shy when she met Kirk and had had so little experience with men, his comments about her appearance were all she had to go on. They were much the same as what her mother had said to her over and over. "Must you have that huge bush of hair flying around your head? Can't you tie it back or something?" She had heard that so many times that tying her hair back was merely habit now.

Brad liked it better down. She let the thought linger in her mind for a moment before she squelched it, annoyed with herself. He hadn't said that at all. He had only said she looked more human. She picked up her brush and worked vigorously for a few minutes until her hair glowed golden brown in the morning light.

Betsy screamed with delight when she saw Elaina. She stood in the crib and jumped up and down, shaking the bars in glee. When Elaina picked her up, the baby hugged her tightly and said, "Mama?" For a minute Elaina allowed herself to pretend.

Harrison sauntered in. In a transport of joy, Betsy flung herself sideways in Elaina's arms, nearly tipping the two of them over. Elaina sat down on the bed abruptly, falling backward onto the crumpled quilt as Harrison hopped up to rub against his new toy, purring. Betsy squealed and giggled, Harrison rubbed and purred, and Elaina simply breathed. Her face turned sideways into the pillow, she drew in a scent at once familiar and unfamiliar, and strangely, deeply exciting. It made her feel light-headed, weak, soft inside, and she quickly rolled away and stood up, carrying Betsy.

"Breakfast," she said. "That's what's needed around here, food. I didn't have any dinner last night."

Betsy seemed to agree, because as soon as she was changed—something that took priority, Elaina realized—she opened her mouth to yell, and began squirting from the fascinating little glands under her tongue. It was a good thing Brad had explained, she thought, or she'd be frantic with worry over it.

Brad . . . Dammit, the man simply wouldn't stay out of her mind. Even while Betsy raged, hammering on the tray of her high chair while Elaina read the instructions on the cereal box and mixed the cereal accordingly, Brad Bradshaw's voice was rumbling through her ears, his scent was tingling her nose, and the memory of how he had felt against her was making her hand shake. Heavens, it made her entire body shake!

She felt her face go hot when she thought of what had happened to his body while they held each other. She knew, of course, about men and morning, but what if it had been because of her? It hadn't been there at first, and then—Oh! Suddenly, she was even more ashamed of herself. The man was a stranger, for heaven's sake! She concentrated hard on getting breakfast into Betsy. Some things, she decided, were best forgotten.

She left the baby playing happily on the floor with Harrison and a chunky plastic bracelet Betsy had seen on her dresser and wanted, while she gathered up the laundry. She stuffed it into the washer, then dashed back to the spare room. She tidied the bed and discovered one pair of large black shoes still neatly tucked under it. She stared at them. Had he left barefoot? She shook her head. The crazy man! Well, it wasn't her problem, was it? So why did she keep wondering about it—and about him—while she quickly ran the vacuum over the carpets.

Her morning routine was shot to pieces and she wasn't sure she liked that. Heavens, she always started work at no later than eight-thirty! Today, she hadn't even made her own bed, the morning paper was sitting out on the doorstep, and her breakfast eggs were still safe in their shells. Well, it would all have to wait. The washer shuddered to a stop, and she hurriedly shifted the wet things into the dryer so she could remake Betsy's bed just in case she needed a nap before Brad came back to get her.

She was struck by a sudden sadness. She didn't want him to take Betsy! Not only that, but without the baby he'd have no reason to return, ever. Of course, that wasn't to say that even if she kept Betsy, he'd come back, but . . . You never knew. *Don't make excuses, Elaina,* she told herself. *If you keep Betsy, it'll be because you like Betsy. But still . . . wouldn't it be nice to have Betsy—and Brad?*

She had just put the vacuum away when she was startled by the welcome sound of the telephone ringing. Leaving Betsy to play in the spare bedroom she dashed to grab the phone in the living room. It was the telephone company informing her that she was all hooked up and ready to go. She thanked the operator politely, and hung up, glad to have her phone in operation. Not that she often called anyone, or that anyone might call her, but it was comforting to know that it was there if she needed it.

"Mama-mama-mama-mama," said Betsy, and Elaina looked down to see her galloping across the hall on hands and knees, making amazingly good time. She crawled right up to Elaina, grabbed two fistfuls of navy wool, and hauled herself upright. "Up," she said very clearly. "Up."

Elaina stared at her and lifted her in her arms. "You talked? You said a word? Oh, Betsy! Betsy, you can talk!" It was wonderful, stupendous! She couldn't believe it! Betsy could talk! She could say more than just "mama." She was a real little person. The idea was so exciting that Elaina wanted to call someone and share the news. But who? No one she knew would care.

No one? One person would. But she couldn't call him to tell him something like that. Could she? No, of course not! She thought about it. She'd say, "Brad, I just had to tell you. Betsy can say 'up.' "

And he'd say, "Lainie! That's great news. I'm glad you called."

Oh, yeah? she asked herself. *Hah!* He'd say "Elaina who? Oh. You. You called me out of surgery to tell me *that*?" Or did emergency room residents do surgery? Whatever, he wouldn't want to be interrupted. He'd hang up, totally disgusted with her and her stupidity. Elaina sighed. She had never felt more lonely in her life.

What would he think of the fact that she had no one to call with exciting news, she wondered, a man who called his mother three times in one month, during nondiscount hours? They must be very close. She sighed again, then lifted her chin determinedly. It wasn't important, she told herself. Some people were close to their families, others were not. That was just the way life was. Letters were what welded her family together, if welded was the word to use for their admittedly loose connection. And those letters were rare, more a touching of bases than news-filled missives.

Thinking about her parents' reaction if she were to call and tell them about Betsy made Elaina smile. Then it made her laugh. Betsy laughed back at her and Elaina gave the baby a hug. It was easy to smile and laugh with Betsy around. Maybe Kirk had been wrong after all. Maybe she would be a good mother. She put such thoughts out of her mind and concentrated on the baby.

"Say it again, honey-bun. Come on, Betsy, say 'up.' " But Betsy was already up. She didn't need to say it again. Instead she said her other word a few more times, then wiggled to get down. "So what did you want up for?" Elaina asked almost complainingly, but she put Betsy on the floor. Maybe Betsy had just felt lonely and had come looking for comfort, she mused. It was nice to have someone come to her for comfort. It was, in a way, comforting.

She remembered her own feeling of loneliness when she realized she had no one to call, and sat on the floor beside Betsy and Harrison. She rolled the bracelet back and forth between them, and they both batted at it. Betsy cooed and kicked her bare feet. Elaina smiled. She wasn't feeling the least bit lonely anymore.

"I'm not going to get any work done today, am I?" she asked presently, thinking how much less eccentric it seemed to be talking to a baby instead of a cat. Which was strange, because the cat likely understood almost as much as the baby did. When she mentioned work to Harrison, he often hopped up on the top edge of her drawing board. This morning, though, he didn't, much preferring to stay where Betsy was. As Elaina did.

Suddenly, she felt amazingly full of energy. But not for work. Today, her studio would remain closed. Outside, the sun was shining and birds were singing and it was a perfect June morning. Babies needed fresh air, didn't they? And milk and more baby food than the few little jars that were left, and some disposable diapers. Betsy had gone through an inordinate number of her cloth ones, and Brad hadn't brought very many at all. If she really did decide to keep Betsy, she'd need more, and soon. So, just in case, she'd buy some.

Scooping up Betsy and the bracelet, she nearly ran to the bathroom. She set the baby and her new toy on the floor. "I need a shower, honey-bun, and coffee and food, and you're going to need lunch soon. But then you and I are going shopping, so you just behave yourself for a few minutes, okay?"

Betsy bit the bracelet, chortled, and pounded with it on the side of the tub. "That's right," said Elaina. "You play with your toys."

Making sure the door was shut tight so Betsy couldn't crawl away and get into trouble somewhere, Elaina stepped into the shower. As she quickly washed, her mind was filled with the things she planned to do with the rest of the time she had Betsy. When she was through and had wrapped a towel around herself and drawn back the shower curtain, though, her mind went totally blank with shock as she saw what trouble Betsy had managed to get into in the confines of the bathroom.

"No! No!" she cried, grabbing the baby and pulling her away from the toilet to safety. She snatched a sodden towel from her wet hands, seeing with horror that she had been sucking on it.

"Oh, Betsy! Betsy! What have you done? What did I let you do?" Frantically, she dried Betsy's face with the end of her own towel, trying to wipe out the baby's mouth, even while she knew that it would do no good. The damage was surely done! Betsy had ingested who knew what number of dreadful germs, horrible microbes, vicious viruses! She needed help! She needed a doctor, and fast!

As if sensing the urgency of the situation, Betsy began to howl energetically, setting Elaina's nerves further on edge. She ran into the living room and grabbed for the telephone, punching the O while she tried to comfort the baby. "Betsy, baby, don't cry. It'll be all right." She wasn't at all sure it would, but knew she had to comfort the screaming child. "I'll get help for you. I'll fix it!

"University Hospital. Emergency," she said to the operator. "Dr. Bradshaw, please. And please hurry!" she cried when a laconic female voice answered.

"Not there? What do you mean, not there? He works there! He has to be there! I need him. This is an emergency!" She was speaking rapidly, almost incoherently, her voice raised to be heard over Betsy's screams. "I need Dr. Bradshaw. Please, please, tell me where he is!"

"I'm right here," said his voice in her ear.

Almost insane with relief, she babbled into the phone. "Oh, Brad, she said you weren't there! It's Betsy. She drank the toilet water and I know she's going to die and her mother entrusted her to my care and I didn't look after her properly and—"

"This is Dr. Bradshaw," he said, taking the phone from her hand and speaking into it. "I'll take care of things." And then he hung it up.

Elaina blinked at him. "You're here!"

"I'm here." He lifted Betsy out of Elaina's arms, ran expert eyes over her, then draped her over his shoulder, patting her back. At once, her squalling stopped. "What happened?" he asked calmly in the sudden stillness.

"She . . . I . . . I left her playing in the bathroom while I was in the shower and she drank toilet water."

He frowned, turned Betsy to face him, and sniffed at her mouth. "She didn't get much, I don't suppose. I don't smell anything."

Elaina glared at him. "Well! I mean, it wasn't exactly—uh—It had been flushed!"

For a moment he gazed at her as if he wasn't sure of what he was hearing, then he shook his head slowly, a grin growing on his face. "Toilet water? You mean, water? Not cologne? Just plain water? Out of the toilet? That's *all*?" And he roared with laughter.

"All?" she echoed, her voice shrill and cutting into his laughter. "All? Isn't it enough? All those germs! She soaked a towel in it and sucked on it! We have to . . . have to disinfect her, or something!"

"Sure," he said, his rich chuckle still rippling out. "You go ahead and disinfect her, Lainie. It'll make you feel better. Sort of like checking her for broken bones."

"You . . . are . . . making . . . fun of me!" she said.

To Brad's horror her face crumpled. He realized she was white and shaking and genuinely frightened. Tears fell from her eyes and she turned from him, her shoulders heaving. Quickly, he set the baby on the floor and gathered the woman close. He led her to the sofa and sat down with her, trying to get her face lifted out of her hands.

Her voice was muffled when she spoke. "I don't know anything about . . . about . . . babies and you know everything and it's not . . . not fair to make fun of me when I was so scared that she was . . . going to d-die and . . . and—"

"Hey, Elaina, take it easy!" He turned her face into the hollow of his shoulder, remembering how it had fit right there early this morning, before he was properly awake. He remembered how fantastic it had felt to hold her then, how he had wanted to walk right back to bed, still holding her, curl his body around hers and—

Oh, lordy! Can that, Bradshaw! He continued patting her back as he had patted Betsy's, feeling the incredible smoothness of her skin under his palm. Hell, this was nothing at all like patting Betsy. "Don't cry, Lainie. I'm sorry." *That's it, keep talking,* he told himself. *Keep your mind on comforting this woman, this stranger, this . . . patient. She needs words now, words that will calm her. Words that will soothe. She doesn't need—*

He swallowed hard and concentrated. "I didn't mean to make fun of you. But it did strike me as funny. All she got was a little bit of clean water. It's no worse than her sucking on a washcloth in the bath. There's nothing there to harm her. I'm sure you're the cleanest person around and I know Betsy is going to be just fine. Come on, now, don't cry any more."

"I never cry," she said, crying harder. She wrapped her arms around his torso and clung to him. "I don't know what's the matter with me!"

Brad felt beads of sweat breaking out on his forehead. He knew damned well what was the matter with *him*! He was holding a nearly naked woman in his arms and responding to the situation the way any red-blooded male would. The sweet scent of her damp hair, the natural perfume of her skin, were getting to him more rapidly than he'd been gotten to in a long, long time. The jutting pressure of her nipples against his chest made him catch his breath and pray for strength.

Think of her as a patient, Bradshaw, he told himself frantically, but the delicious warmth of her body told him this was no patient. This was a wonderful armful of woman he wanted to hold closer and closer, tighter and tighter. He wanted to get rid of that towel she was wrapped in. He wanted . . .

He wanted his hand to stop rubbing her back, but it seemed to have a will of its own. It slowed, moving in circles, as he tested the satin of her skin. He traced her spine right down to where the towel was loosely wrapped. His breathing became labored. His chest constricted. His other hand came into play, caressing her shoulder, feeling the delicacy of the bones under the skin. His fingers massaged, sliding along the curve of flesh that led to her slender neck, tangling in the softness of her hair. God, she felt good! When was the last time a woman had stirred him like this? He couldn't remember. Maybe never. He'd thought he was too tired these past couple of years to be turned on. How wrong he had been!

This woman was turning him on as if he were a green kid who'd never held a naked female before. She was soft and sweet and delicately made, in spite of her height. Her height? She fit him perfectly.

She had gone motionless in his arms, her weeping quieted, her face still hidden in the hollow of his shoulder. He could feel the dampness of her tears on his shirt. She caught her breath as he cupped a hand under her chin, then he was gazing into her eyes. They were the same gray as he'd remembered, but not so serene now. They were nearly silver, with dark rings around the irises, huge and moist and incredibly lovely within their wet, dark lashes. Slightly wary, those eyes gazed back at him, filled with the same questions that were battering at his own consciousness, questions he had no intention of even thinking about now, questions he didn't want her to have a chance to ask herself or voice aloud. Her cheeks were faintly flushed and her lips were parted, pink and soft, and he didn't want to waste time on thought or discussion. Action was what he craved. And those lips.

He tilted her face higher, lowered his head, and took those soft pink lips gently, almost reverently. He felt them tremble and part under his urging to admit the tip of his tongue. Slowly, delicately, he tasted her. He found her sweeter than he had imagined a woman could taste, and ran his tongue along the inside of her lower lip. A tremor there translated itself into a shudder that quaked through her whole body, and her nipples peaked against his chest. He felt his own body surge in a deep response of its own.

He wanted to crush her in his arms and deepen the kiss, to take it to its logical conclusion, but the memory of those drenched gray eyes gazing at him with such a world of questions in them held him back. He lifted his head reluctantly, watching her face.

Slowly, her long lashes fluttered up and she looked at him, bemused. She blinked as if she didn't know quite where she was, and levered herself away from his chest. With his hands on her shoulders, he helped her sit erect, suddenly becoming aware that her towel had slipped down to expose her perfect breasts. His gaze fell to those creamy orbs with their delicate, rosy tips, and one hand followed, almost of its own volition. Gently, gently, he brushed the backs of his fingers up the underside of the curve. He watched her eyes widen and darken, then fill with realization of what was happening.

She snatched up her towel, wrapping it tightly around herself as she shot to her feet. "Don't!" she gasped, although he was no longer doing anything at all except looking. And then she was gone, her long, slim legs taking great strides as she fled to the safety of her bedroom.

Four

For the third time, Elaina told herself that she couldn't stay in her bedroom forever. She drew a deep breath, put her hand on the doorknob, and briskly turned it. She was neatly dressed in a pair of navy slacks and a white blouse with long sleeves and a high collar. Her hair was pinned into its tidy bun at the nape of her neck, and she should have felt ready to face the world. But what she felt was nervous and diffident and still deeply shaken by that kiss.

Brad was in the utility room, taking Betsy's clothes from the dryer and stuffing them into a bag. If he even remembered that kiss and the rest of it, he showed no sign.

"What are you doing?" she asked.

"Packing up Betsy's stuff."

She stared at him. She shook her head. She weakly said, "Oh . . ." and leaned on the doorjamb. "Right now?"

"You said only one night." He scarcely looked at her. When the clothes were all in, he set the bag on the floor and crowded past her. Elaina followed him to the spare room. Betsy was there, rump high, on the bare crib mattress, asleep.

"Where are you taking her?"

"We found a foster home for her," he said, gathering up the few bits of clothing Betsy hadn't worn yet. Elaina nodded, swallowed hard, and reached into the crib to touch Betsy's downy hair.

"What if I . . . changed my mind? What if I decided I . . . want her here?"

"Have you changed your mind?"

"Her own mother wanted me to have her."

He gave her an all-encompassing look that told her he was likening her to Miss Harris again. "Her mother probably has no idea the woman she chose hides behind her hair."

Elaina tilted her chin proudly. "If I were hiding behind my hair," she said, "I'd hardly pull it back, would I?"

He grinned. "Wouldn't you?"

"No. And the way I wear my hair is none of your business. Nor do I think it has anything to do with how well I could care for Betsy." He continued to look at her, no longer grinning, but with a hint of laughter deep in his eyes.

She felt oddly compelled to say something more. "How is she? Margo Lawrence?"

He sat on the end of the single bed, his expression bleak and sad. "I could say she's holding her own. It would be true. But all I can think of is that we're doing everything possible for her, have been for nearly twenty-four hours, and there is still no appreciable change."

He fiddled with the zipper of the pink-and-blue diaper bag, not looking at Elaina. For the moment, she could study him undetected. He had found another pair of shoes and had changed out of the crumpled clothing he'd slept in, although his cotton pants and short-sleeved knit shirt might have been used the same way. Either that, or he had just dragged them on as they came out of the dryer. Really, the man needed someone to look after him, she thought. Obviously he didn't get enough sleep and last night he had said he was too tired to be hungry. He also worried about his patients. No one should live under that kind of stress. He was a doctor. Didn't he know that?

He glanced up and caught her staring. She turned away quickly, feeling her face go warm, and wished futilely that she didn't have such give-away skin.

"What are you thinking?" he asked.

Before she could stop herself, she blurted out, "That you're exhausted and look as if you're about to fall asleep on that bed again."

He got to his feet and shook his head. "Don't worry. I won't do that to you twice." He stubbed his toe on something, bent, and saw his shoes. "So there they are! I wondered where I had left them."

"Do you always go out on emergency calls without your shoes?"

He shrugged. "Sometimes. If I'm not fully awake. But since I live right in the hospital, it doesn't usually matter. And speaking of the hospital, I have to get back. I'm on duty, but someone's covering for me while I take care of things for Betsy. You really want to keep her?"

"Yes," she said. "For as long as necessary." There was no doubt in her mind anymore. She looked down at the sleeping baby and forgot everything but Betsy. Betsy who needed her. Betsy who cuddled up to her when she was lonely. Betsy who alleviated her own loneliness in doing so.

"Okay," he said. "And thanks. I wasn't looking forward to telling Margo when she regains consciousness that Betsy was somewhere else."

He moved toward her, carrying his black shoes, and Elaina backed nervously out of the room. They walked to the front door and just before he opened it, she said, "She will regain consciousness, won't she?"

"I hope so, Lainie. But there are no guarantees in medicine. We have the best specialists available over there at the hospital, and they're doing everything possible. They're pretty helpless, though, without a history from her, and she was in no shape to give us one. We don't know much more than her name and address and that she's Betsy's mother. She does housework for people, but we don't know who those people might be. We don't know where she's from, or who Betsy's father is, or if Margo has parents somewhere worrying about her, people who might be able to help us find out what's wrong.

"When I went to her apartment to get Betsy's things, the landlady said she'd only lived there a couple of months. There wasn't much food in the place other than baby food and milk, and Margo's in a dangerously run-down condition. God, she's just a kid herself. I'd be surprised if she were over eighteen." He pounded one fist into the opposite hand. "Damn, but I hate this helplessness!"

"I'm sorry," Elaina said softly. "I know it worries you."

"Damn right it worries me! It happens too often. But Betsy's one of the lucky ones. Do you know that poverty and malnourishment are believed by many experts to be the number one killers of babies in this country? *This* country! Where we live so well. Sure, some of those deaths are attributed to other causes, but the root cause in so many cases is just plain poverty. And you can't blame the parents," he went on, as if she might have been going to do that. "When the paycheck, be it earnings from a job or welfare from the government, isn't enough, it simply isn't enough. There is no way to stretch it. The clothes I brought yesterday . . . well, that's it. That is Betsy's entire wardrobe. And poor little Margo has even less. The two of them share a foam pad for a bed. That may be all right this time of year, but what about winter when it's cold and drafty and the few blankets the two of them have aren't enough?"

Elaina raised her brows. "Then where did all the baby furniture come from?"

"I . . . uh . . . There's a fund for things like that," he said, his eyes sliding away from hers. Quickly, he wrenched open the door. "I'll be back," he said, and before she could ask him when, he was gone. This time he made it off the porch successfully, even though he missed the steps again. He slammed the gate, and the sound reverberated in the warm air.

Sure there was a fund, she thought, staring at the empty street after the green van had gone. And that fund came right out of his own hip pocket.

She wondered what residents earned and didn't think it was a whole lot. She closed the door and went back inside, remembering again that she hadn't yet had breakfast.

"Hello," said Terri Greenspan, Elaina's next door neighbor. She stood up from her weeding as Elaina pushed Betsy in the stroller past her driveway. "The boys told me you had a baby. I thought they were just romancing the way they do. They're very imaginative. Did you adopt?"

"No. No, I'm just looking after a friend's child for a few days."

"She's a real sweetheart. What's her name?" Elaina told her and Terri went on, "The boys are thrilled to have an artist whose name they've seen on so many of their books living next door. I've told them not to bother you, but I've seen them in your yard. I hope they aren't too much trouble. Kick them out whenever you want. I won't be offended. I'm sure you need peace to work."

Betsy bounced, trying to make the stroller go. "No, they've been okay," Elaina assured Terri. "I know they're interested in what I do."

"Still, you don't have to put up with them when you're busy. They're curious, of course, and they miss the Wilton kids who used to live in your house. I think they expected that our next neighbors would automatically provide them with new buddies. This is a strange neighborhood. Some years there are too many kids, other years, not enough. The other day I heard someone describe it as a community of the newly wed or nearly dead."

Elaina smiled and said that she didn't think that she or Terri qualified for either description.

"No, we don't, and for that reason we should stick together. Why don't you come in and have a cup of coffee with me? I could do with a break from this infernal weeding."

Elaina was surprised to find herself actually thinking about it. Coffee with neighbors was not something she'd ever done, or thought she might want to. But Betsy made the decision for her, bouncing harder and shaking the stroller as if urging it to move forward. She had sat long enough. If she could have said "Go!" she would have.

"Thanks," Elaina said, "but I think I'd better keep Betsy in motion. Another time, though, I'd like to." As she said it, she discovered it was true.

"Sure thing," Terri said cheerfully, and gave Betsy a little wave of her fingers, saying "Bye-bye."

While Elaina stared in astonishment, Betsy waved her fat little hand. She didn't say anything, but she didn't have to. Her hand spoke for her. Feeling vastly proud of Betsy's accomplishment, Elaina walked on through splotches of sunshine into deep coves of shade from the huge, leafy trees that lined the boulevard. She remembered that she hadn't told Brad—Dr. Bradshaw—that Betsy could now say two words.

It didn't matter, she thought. She could tell him later. Later. It was a long time since she'd had something like another person's arrival to look forward to. It was a fine and novel experience, but she cautioned herself sternly not to get too used to it. Because, of course, he was only coming to check on Betsy, and when Betsy's mother recovered there would be no more need for him to come. Unless he came to see her.

Now why had she thought of that? There wasn't much likelihood of anything like that. He wasn't what might be considered a man in her life. She didn't need one, or want one. She was a self-sufficient adult who could look after herself quite well, and had done so for a long time. So why, she wondered, had it felt so good when he'd held her in his arms this morning? Why had she let her own arms go around him? And why had she cried?

Because she was hungry, she admonished herself quickly. Low blood sugar. Didn't that make people feel weepy and weak and unable to cope? Of course it did. Then why had she responded to his kiss the way she had? What had that to do with hunger? *Oh, dummy,* she thought, bumping the stroller down over a curb. *That was hunger too. But hunger of a different sort altogether.*

In three years, no man had affected her the way Brad Bradshaw had this morning. The feel of him against her body, the scent of his skin and hair and clothing, the sound of his voice rumbling in his chest, had touched something deep within her, something she thought had died, or at least gone far away. But it hadn't, had it? It had only been waiting for someone like him to bring it back into the open. The thought of its being exposed again, like a raw nerve, frightened her.

Only it hadn't felt like a raw nerve. It had felt good, better than she remembered, and for several minutes after her tears had stopped she had simply lain there against his chest, absorbing the goodness, letting the pleasure caused by his hands on her bare skin wash through her in taller and taller waves until she was dizzy. When he had tilted up her face and kissed her, she had had no thought of trying to stop what was happening to her.

At times with Kirk she had experienced sensations similar to the ones she'd felt this morning. But she knew instinctively that those sensations were only the beginning of what she was capable of feeling, that there was more, much more, and that one day she would find it.

She hadn't found it with Kirk.

Could she find it with Brad?

With a shake of her head, Elaina put a stop to such crazy thoughts. He had kissed her to offer comfort and that was all. When he had touched her breasts the way he had, caressing them with his hand and his eyes, what had that been for?

She didn't know and refused to dwell on it. She had shopping to do.

In the supermarket she carefully fastened Betsy into a shopping cart and proceeded down the first aisle. Shopping was fairly routine until the time came to buy the things she had never bought before.

Baby cereal was on sale. She chose a few boxes. Those jars of food were so small that they took up hardly any room in the cart. Peaches. She knew Betsy liked those. *So does Brad,* said a little voice inside her, but she pretended not to hear it. Leaning forward, she kissed Betsy on the top of her head. If peaches were good, why not apricots, and apple-raspberry combination? The other glop Betsy had enjoyed had been a mixture of meat and vegetables. She selected a variety of those, too, and stacked them in the cart. She avoided liver with anything. Nothing, she thought, would make liver palatable, and anyone who forced it on an innocent baby should be shot. Milk. Yes. They'd need plenty of that, she thought, smiling at Betsy who was kicking her with short, fat bare toes.

In the sundries aisle, she picked up some plastic bibs with kittens and bunnies on them and a package of six baby bottles in case something happened to one of Betsy's two, and a couple of boxes of diapers. There was even an amazing assortment of baby clothes there, but she didn't like the quality. She'd check out the children's store she had seen every time she walked through the mall. Elaina smiled to herself. Betsy was going to have some new clothes today. This was turning out to be fun.

It wasn't quite as much fun when she saw the total on the cash register, but she asked herself what else she had to spend her money on. There was nothing she wanted more than to get Betsy what she needed. And among the things she needed was a dry diaper. Taking three out of one of the boxes, Elaina arranged to have the rest of her purchases delivered. Then for the first time in her life she learned what the interior of the baby-change room looked like.

In the children's store, she discovered that there were a great many things that Betsy didn't have that seemed absolutely essential. Among them were a clown that sang when she wound up its red nose like a key, and an apple that, when rolled across the floor, made a pleasant tinkling sound. But what Betsy seemed to like best was a huge green rubber cucumber that squeaked when she bit it.

There were clothes, of course, and the selection was amazing. Who'd have thought that designers would come up with so many different styles for babies and small children? It was really a temptation to take one of everything, but Elaina restrained herself. After all, how many outfits could one baby wear?

She did indulge herself with a sweet little parasol that clipped onto the handle of Betsy's stroller and cast a circle of shade to keep the sun off that tender skin. And Betsy did need shoes, didn't she? Brad hadn't brought any with the clothing he'd found for her in Margo's apartment.

Having arranged for those purchases to be delivered, too, Elaina continued on down the mall, gazing in windows as she went. For no good reason that she could think of, she soon found herself standing at the edge of a department store's lingerie department, gazing at the mannequins, wondering how she would look in that incredibly sexy soft pink teddy with all the lace. Or in that peach-colored nightie with the skinny straps, slinky and silky and shockingly sheer. Why, at the age of thirty-one, she was still wearing the same kind of underwear and nightwear that her mother had bought for her, she simply did not know. Of course, when she was with Kirk, they had been saving too hard—or she had—to want to spend money on such luxuries. And he hadn't cared what she wore, as long as it was clean and covered her decently.

Besides, Kirk had never really looked at her anyway, so it couldn't have mattered what she wore.

She moved on past the lingerie reluctantly, shivering as she remembered the very appreciative look in Brad Bradshaw's eyes when he stroked her naked breast. He had liked the way she looked. He had. She knew it.

Abruptly, she spun the stroller and herself in a one-eighty and strode back the way she had come.

Moments later, she stuffed the bag containing her purchases down deep in the carrying pouch of the stroller and left in a rush, knowing she was on the verge of changing her mind.

Crazy, she told herself. *You are crazy, Elaina McIvor! Take them back. You'll never need to wear them!*

But she couldn't get rid of the little voice that kept whispering, *"What if?"* in her ear.

After one more stop in a bookstore where she stocked up on everything from Dr. Spock to the latest, most modern views on child care, Elaina headed home with the new umbrella tilted jauntily to keep the sun out of the baby's eyes.

Betsy smiled and cooed and laughed, and kicked her feet so the bells on her new shoes jingled. Strangers smiled at the pair of them. Elaina smiled back. She felt happier than she had been in more than three years. No, happier than she had been in her entire adult life, she thought. Today had given her more pleasure than she could have imagined.

The sun was warm and the scent of newly mown grass and roses and honeysuckle hung in the soft air. Elaina wanted to dance. She wanted to sing.

Betsy did both, her face wreathed in smiles as Elaina bent low over the handle of the stroller and said, "Boo!" every few paces. The baby's gurgles of delight were infectious. Elaina laughed along with her, picking up her pace, going faster and faster, feeling wilder and wilder, floating higher and higher on a cloud of euphoria like none she had ever ridden before, until suddenly she was snatched back to earth by a loud, piping voice. "Hey, Billy, look at that! Miss McIby is hippety-hoppin'!"

Miss McIby is hippety-hoppin'!

The squeaky, disbelieving voice shocked Elaina into an awareness of where she was and what she was doing. By golly, yes, she was hippety-hopping! Feeling her face turn bright red, she bent her head down and let her hair fall forward, most definitely hiding behind it this time. Oh, Lord! How long had she been doing that? The whole block? More than one block? All the way home? She had no idea, but was aghast that she had even hippetied for one single hop! Lord! What was the matter with her?

She was so intent on keeping her head down and her face hidden so that none of the neighbors would recognize her, she didn't see the large pair of feet in white canvas shoes until she ran the front wheels of her stroller right up onto them.

"Hey, Miss McIby, you look cute hippety-hopping," Brad said, and she covered her eyes with her hand. Was there to be no end to her humiliation? Did he have to be here? Didn't he ever work at that hospital? "I'm glad you took your hair down again," he went on. "It bounces real nice." He lowered his voice. "Among other things."

She groaned and backed the stroller off his toes, then uncovered her eyes to meet his dancing green gaze.

She almost laughed, but choked back the impulse. This was just too embarrassing.

"Don't be ashamed of having fun, Lainie," he said softly. He pushed her hair back on one side and tucked it behind her ear; his touch was a lingering caress that she continued to feel long after his hand was back at his side. "I had a lot of fun watching you. And Bitsy-Bet loved it. I heard you both laughing before you turned the corner."

That answered one question, anyway. She had hippetied more than one hop. A lot more, probably. Suddenly, she was suppressing a giggle. She bit her lip.

"Go ahead," he urged her. "You can laugh at yourself, you know. There's no sin in having a sense of humor."

She did laugh. She couldn't help it. What she had done was ridiculous, and inappropriate for a woman of thirty-one, but he didn't seem to be judging her. The little boys had disappeared somewhere so she could lean on Brad and laugh until she nearly cried. Oh, she must have looked very funny indeed, because now that she was laughing, so was he. He was leaning on her even as he propped her up, right out there on the public sidewalk outside her yard. When they both sobered and she backed away from him, he reached out and ruffled her hair. "Good for you." His praise was nice to hear.

She smiled at him and wiped her eyes on the back of her hand. "What are you doing here?" she asked. "Aren't you supposed to work?"

"I'm doing a split shift today. I don't go back on until eleven tonight. I came to see Betsy and ask if you'd like to go out for dinner. Nothing fancy. Just some place where we can take the baby. I thought you might be worn out from your unaccustomed job." He chuckled, taking the stroller from her and pushing it through the gate. "I guess I was wrong."

"You don't have to worry about me," she said gruffly, trying not to feel touched that he had done just that. "And you don't have to take me out for dinner." He looked too tired to go anywhere but to bed.

"Good," he said, picking up baby and stroller and setting them on the porch. "Then that means I'm invited for dinner here."

Five

Elaina stared at him and shook her head. "I didn't mean that at all," she said, mounting the steps and fumbling with her key.

He looked so crestfallen she had to smile. She fought an insane impulse to ruffle his hair as he had done to hers. "But if you're hungry, Dr. Bradshaw, I'm sure I can find something to fill you up."

"You called me Brad before," he said, wheeling Betsy inside.

Only in her own mind, she knew. "When?"

"On the phone." He lifted Betsy out of the stroller and stood her in the center of the coffee table, admiring her new shoes while she hung onto his thumbs and danced. Elaina started pulling books out of the carrying pouch in the back of her stroller and came across her bag of lingerie. She stuffed it down behind a chair, knowing she was turning pink as she did so. "No, I didn't. I've never talked to you on the phone."

He looked askance at the first half-dozen books she set on the other end of the coffee table. "Sure you did. Or you thought you did. But I was here, having walked in through your unlocked door when I heard you screaming and Betsy howling. Remember? And you should never leave your door unlocked."

She remembered. She felt her face go warmer as she remembered. His arms. His kiss. Her towel.

He had the bad manners to comment. "Now, what's that blush for?" he asked. When she ignored his question, he went on, "You have the clearest skin I have ever seen, Lainie, and I like the way it signals your emotions. Blushing's a neat trick for a woman to have."

She shot him a sharp look. "Trick? Do you think I can control it? I only wish I could, so I could stop it! And my name, in case you are having trouble remembering, is Elaina!"

He looked uncomfortable. "I'm sorry. I didn't put that very well. I didn't mean trick as in subterfuge. I meant you look very pretty when you blush, Elaina."

"Oh." It pleased her inordinately to hear him say that, yet she didn't know where to look. She only knew that her face was turning pink again. Dammit, the overuse they were getting, it was a wonder her capillaries didn't simply explode! "Thank you."

She didn't know if she was thanking him for the compliment or for pronouncing her name properly for once.

"What in the world did you buy all these books for?" he asked, when they were all stacked on the table. He set Betsy on the carpet and she began to cry. Picking her up, he checked her bottom, then held her away from himself, nose wrinkled.

"I bought them to learn a few things," Elaina answered. "So I don't have to call for help when I'm in doubt, like I did today."

He grinned. "I don't think you'd have taken the time to look something like that up in a book. You were in such a panic you wouldn't have been able to read."

She glowered at him. "You still think it's funny, don't you?"

"I don't think your fear was funny. I laughed this morning because I didn't realize at first how badly scared you were. But yes, I do think the incident was funny, and when you think about it, I believe you'll agree. Meantime, this little girl needs clean pants." He picked up one of the remaining diapers that Elaina had taken out of the pouch and marched away, still holding Betsy at arm's length.

In spite of herself, Elaina did smile. He was right. She'd been in too much of a panic to be reasonable. All she had been able to do was react. Okay, so she had overreacted. She had behaved like a fool again.

She stacked the books neatly by size and picked up the top one. She stared at the first page as she listened to Brad making silly noises and spouting nonsense words to Betsy. He never seemed to mind making a fool of himself, she thought. It must be nice to be so self-confident. Maybe by the time she had read all those books she'd be a little more that way, at least with Betsy. Diligently, she began to scan the first book. She skipped over the chapters on pregnancy and infancy and went right to the part about development from ten to twelve months. Waving bye-bye and saying single words weren't considered uncommon at that age, and were by no means indicative of genius.

She slammed the book shut in disgust. What did P.T. Nelson, Ph.D., know, anyway? He probably never got nearer to a baby than he did to the moon. Sat there in an isolated little lab somewhere and did experiments with monkeys or something.

"Hey, Lainie! Lainie!" Brad came tearing out of Betsy's room carrying her astride his hip, his face split by a huge smile. "She said 'up.' She reached out her arms to me and said 'up.' Isn't she smart?"

There! she thought, mentally thumbing her nose at Dr. Nelson. A real baby-expert thinks our baby is pretty smart. Which, of course, she was.

"I know," Elaina said, beaming. "She came crawling out of her bedroom this morning and climbed up my bathrobe and asked me to pick her up. Come on, honey-bun, say it again." She took Betsy, who was reaching for her, and set her down on the floor. "Up, Betsy? Up?" But Betsy wasn't interested in getting up. Harrison had come to pay homage. They let the cat and baby play together for a few minutes until Betsy began to rub her eyes and whine.

"Nap time," Elaina said, and carried her off to bed.

While she was settling Betsy, the doorbell rang and she heard Brad admit the boy from the supermarket. Load after load came in, and in the kitchen Elaina found Brad surrounded by brown paper bags, plastic sacks, and jars and jars of baby food.

He was aghast. "Nobody buys baby food in these quantities," he said. "You buy a few jars at a time. It's going to take her three years to go through all this, and long before that she'll have teeth and be eating ordinary food. You have to send it back, Elaina."

"Don't exaggerate. It won't take her anything like three years." There wasn't *that* much, she thought. More than she had remembered, now that she saw it all spread out, but still, Betsy would eat it. If not here, then when she went home again. The thought left Elaina feeling hollow.

"You may as well open a day-care center," Brad said, trying to find room in the cupboards for all the packages of cereal. "This is crazy! Did you get anything for you to eat? Ah, yes, I see you did. Eggs and cheese and canned shrimp. Fine. You can pack your arteries full of cholesterol and have a heart attack by the time you're fifty. You'll be too weak to chew and we can feed you all the leftover baby food."

Elaina laughed and handed him a big plastic bag. "Grown-up food," she said.

"Good." He delved into the bag and pulled out a small roast of beef, a package of chicken breasts, and some cod fillets. "Which one for dinner? Remember, I invited myself."

She remembered. She also remembered that she had seconded the invitation. She wished she could recant it when he put the beef and fish into the freezer and held the chicken out for her to see. "How about this?" he asked, his eyes twinkling with an unholy light. "I like breasts." She compressed her lips and turned away quickly, but not before he laughed at her flushed face. She knew perfectly well that he knew she was remembering what had happened this morning. She bit her lip. Thinking about it sent little flames through her body. She didn't want to think at all, but the memory persisted, growing more and more intrusive each time she found him looking at her. Because he was nearly always looking at her lips—or her breasts.

She unpacked the vegetables and loaded them into the drawers of the refrigerator, crowding past him as he folded bags. Each time she had to brush close to him in the small kitchen she became more aware of him. Was he deliberately getting in her way? she wondered. When she was trying to slip the folded bags onto a high shelf, he reached over her head and took them from her, cornering her. Maybe it was only an accident that the length of his body rested against hers, warming her with its heat, setting her heart to racing as she caught the same tangy scent as had been on the pillow he'd used in the night. His hand on her shoulder as he steadied himself was as evocative as the touch of his palm on her bare skin this morning, and she felt his fingers move as if he, too, were remembering. She held very still as wave after wave of heat rushed through her, but then he was gone, stepping back from her while she clung to the side of the stove and hoped he hadn't noticed her trembling knees.

When she was able to turn around, she expected to see him watching her, laughing. Instead, he had gone back to folding bags as if nothing at all had happened. Probably nothing had. To him.

He shook out the long, curling cash register tape from one bag and unrolled it over his hand. His eyes grew wider and wider as he scanned it.

"Holy cow!" he exclaimed when he reached the bottom line. He looked at her. "That little shopping spree cost you a bundle, didn't it?"

She shrugged. "Groceries don't come cheap. I don't suppose you buy many, living in the hospital the way you do. What's it like, living there? Can you do any cooking for yourself or do you have to eat hospital food all the time?"

He was not to be distracted. "You can't possibly afford all this," he said, reaching for his wallet. "I'd like to share Betsy's expenses with you."

She pushed his wallet away and snatched the tape from his hand. "No," she said sharply. She tore the tape into small pieces, then dropped them into the garbage can. "There's a fund for things like this, Doctor," she added gently. It amused her to see him turn that interesting shade of brick once more. And he teased her about blushing. Didn't he know he did it too? She kept her speculations to herself, changing the subject.

"How's Margo?" She had hesitated to ask in case the news was bad, not wanting to depress him again if he had managed to leave his worries behind for once. She liked it better when his eyes smiled as they had been doing ever since he'd seen her hippety-hopping down the sidewalk. To her relief, his smile didn't fade. It grew, and he looked less weary.

"A little better. Her temperature's dropped half a point and held like that since early this afternoon."

"I'm glad," she said softly.

"Me, too, but now can we go back to what we were talking about? I don't want to think about patients for the next"—he glanced at his watch, a utilitarian, stainless steel job with a sweep second hand—"the next six hours and fifty-three minutes."

And she didn't want to talk about what they had been discussing. She was about to tell him so when the doorbell shrilled its nasty sound again and she ran to answer it, not wanting it to wake Betsy.

It was the delivery from the children's store.

Brad sat down on the sofa and sighed, looking at the baby clothes she had bought. Like the baby food, there was more here than was strictly necessary. All was of the finest quality, as were the toys. He wound the clown's nose and listened to the remarkably clear voice singing "Rock-a-bye, Baby" and set it down again, watching Elaina's bright face.

She was in her glory, unfolding and checking each garment for at least the third time, admiring it, adoring it. Holding up a little red jumpsuit, she turned it around for him to see the back of it. "Look at the pockets," she said, her face aglow. "Isn't that just the cutest thing you've ever seen? I mean, pockets! What's she going to put in them?"

"Joy," he said.

"Pardon me?" She tilted her head to one side. "Did you say 'joy'?"

He smiled. "Something my mom says to kids who put their hands in their pockets. Pockets are for keeping your joy in. If you plug them up with hands, there's no room for joy. I still find myself snatching my hands out of my pockets whenever I catch them in there."

Elaina smiled. "I like that. And I'm glad I bought Betsy something with pockets for her to keep her joy in. Oh, I had so much fun doing this!"

She was sitting cross-legged on the floor, her gray eyes shining, a smile on her wide pink mouth. He reached out to grab a handful of hair at the back of her head and tugged gently until she came up onto her knees before him.

"Lainie . . ." He groaned softly, his breath feathering across her face. "Lainie?"

"What?" she asked, staring into his eyes, forgetting to remind him of what her name really was.

"This," he murmured. He gently covered her mouth with his, his tongue just barely stroking the tiny gap between her lips. It widened enough for him to penetrate and slide slickly along the sensitive inner skin of her bottom lip. She made a slight sound and her lips parted farther. Swiftly, he dipped inside her mouth, his tongue tangling with hers, coaxing it to respond. Then he withdrew to kiss the corners of her mouth, to stroke along the outline of her lips, setting loose a deep pulsing throb of longing within her.

With his free hand he touched the small of her back, bringing her closer, in between his knees. He massaged her spine with the tips of his fingers, feeling the tremors that ran through her body, feeling her softening as she began to respond. Her tongue darted against his and her breathing deepened, quickened, keeping pace with his. Again he felt that rushing surge of need that had nearly overcome him this morning. Again, he wanted to sweep her into a full embrace, crush her to him, feel her under him, surrounding him, surrendering to him. . . .

He tore his mouth from hers and dropped his hand from her hair, letting her go. "I had to do that," he said huskily.

A sigh shuddered from her as she sat back on her heels and gazed up at him. Her chest was heaving under the thin fabric of her blouse. "What for?" she whispered.

"Because." He shifted on the sofa, uncomfortably aware of how much kissing her had aroused him. "Because you are a very nice person and I like you. And because . . ."

He couldn't move his gaze from her face, from those huge, luminous eyes that shone with a light unlike any he had ever seen. He didn't believe that she had to ask why he had kissed her. She knew how lovely she was. She knew how she could get to a man with her long, sleek body in those damned virginal clothes. Those pleated navy pants were tight only at their buttoned cuffs, hinting at the shape under them, and that high-necked, nunlike blouse made her softly rounded breasts all the more tantalizing. Or did she only get to him because he knew just how long and slim those legs were, how those breasts looked with their jutting rose-colored nipples waiting for his touch? He tore his gaze from her, studying the nap of the carpet, his shoes, the holes where the laces went through. As long as he didn't look at her, maybe he'd be all right.

"Because what?" she asked.

"Just because," he said, beginning to recover some of his equilibrium. He dared to meet her eyes again. "Just because you tasted so good this morning and I had to know if you still did."

"Oh." She wouldn't ask him. Couldn't ask him. She could only look at him, wondering.

"You do," he said finally.

"I didn't ask!" She laughed self-consciously.

He smiled. "You didn't have to."

He stood and reached down a hand to help her up. She pulled away quickly, moving to the far side of the room to check Brahms, to see if he had fully recovered from yesterday's trauma.

"Why did you take your hair down?" he asked from close behind her. He feathered his fingers through its fineness. It was like gossamer, he thought. "Angel hair," he murmured.

She moved away again, this time sitting in a high-backed chair with an ottoman in front of it. She hitched up her knees and put her toes on the ottoman.

"I—" She frowned. "I just wanted to."

She was sure he saw through her, certain he knew she had done it because of what he had said. But he didn't comment further on that subject. He sat on the ottoman and smoothed the frown from between her brows with a gentle thumb, then combed his fingers through the hair at her temple.

"Don't frown so much. Smile," he ordered, and she jerked away from his hand.

"Please, don't keep touching me."

"Why not?"

"I—I'm not used to being touched."

"But you don't hate it."

Damn him, he knew she didn't. She moved restlessly, hooking her heels up against the front of the chair cushion. Her mother would have heartily disapproved. "I told you. I'm just not used to it. You . . . you're a very physical person, aren't you? You seem to need to be touching all the time."

"Not all the time," he said. "And not all people. But yes, I guess you could say that I am a very physical man. And I like to touch you. So get used to it."

"Why should I?" she asked challengingly, getting to her feet and sidling away from him. "The liking would have to be mutual for me to get used to it."

"Are you telling me the liking's not mutual?"

She met his gaze for a moment, then shook her head. "I didn't say I didn't like it. Only that I'm not used to it. And now, if you'll excuse me, I have to get some work done while Betsy's asleep. I have a deadline that I'll miss if I don't try to keep up."

"Are you kicking me out?"

She hesitated. "No. You could sit with me if it wouldn't bore you. I don't talk much when I'm working," she added by way of warning.

"I won't be bored."

The room he followed her into was large, with windows on two sides and sliding doors leading to a patio. It was furnished mostly in wicker, but was dominated by a tilted drawing table and a high stool. Two angled lamps clamped to the top of the table provided shadow-free light, and an array of pens and inks and pencils stood on a flat table nearby.

"This room is what prompted me to buy a house that was much too large for one woman and a cat," she said, noticing his gaze sweeping the area. "I couldn't resist all the lovely natural light that pours in here from morning to evening."

"I can understand that." He walked to the glass doors and looked out at the patio. Tubs of red geraniums surrounded its perimeter, and a broad assortment of hanging plants were suspended from the open beam structure overhead, forming a jungle of color and texture with patterns of sun and shade for contrast. Beyond the patio was a large, secluded lawn surrounded by a high laurel hedge. The grass needed cutting, he noticed, but the flower beds were lush and neatly weeded.

He turned from the garden to watch while Elaina set up paper and pens and small pots of different colored inks. She worked quickly, efficiently, her long-fingered hands never awkward, never hesitant, and then she was drawing, her concentration so deep that he knew she had forgotten him. He didn't mind, and took the opportunity to study her. But looking at her made him think and thinking made him . . . He slipped outside, found an old push mower, and cut the grass.

Elaina found that she worked jerkily at first, so aware was she of Brad's presence. She had never had that problem with Kirk. Indeed, she had all too often used her work to block him out, or at least to block out her concerns about the paucity of feeling in their marriage. Eventually, though, Brad's quiet, unobtrusive presence ceased to impinge on her consciousness, and she slipped into the semitrance of drawing. The outside world was only dimly noticed. She was hardly disturbed when she heard Brad mowing the lawn, then later, getting Betsy up.

She did stop working, though, leaning back and stretching as she listened to Brad show Betsy her new toys.

"Why don't you bring her in here to play?" she called out.

Brad gathered up baby and toys, happy to return to the restful, bright room where Elaina sat perched on her tall stool.

"What is that?" he asked, leaning over her shoulder to peer at what she was drawing. She quivered at the scent of him as he bent close, but managed to answer evenly enough.

"That," she said with a grimace, "is a turtle with sails."

He grinned. "Interesting concept. Why does the turtle require sails? What kind of a story is this, anyway?"

She shrugged. "I guess you'd call it a preschool fantasy. It starts out, 'Most pets are so boring. There are dogs, there are cats. And goldfish, and hamsters. Why can't we have bats?' "

"I like it. And it's a darned good question. What comes next?"

She opened a drawer in a nearby cabinet and pulled out a stack of pages already bearing neat drawings and lettering. He took them and read aloud as he leafed through them: " 'Or red and white zebras, or midget-size whales. Or worms that can sing . . .' " He glanced at the drawing on her table and nodded. "Of course. 'Or turtles with sails.' " Flipping back through, he said, "I like your whale spouting in the bathtub, squirting the child's fat belly. You're very, very good, aren't you?" he asked, and it wasn't a rhetorical question at all. He waited for an answer.

"Let's say I'm successful and enjoy what I'm doing. As to being good, I'll only consider myself that as long as I remain successful."

"Fair enough," he said. "How many books have you illustrated?"

She inked in a bright blue triangle on the geometrically patterned spinnaker swooping out from the mast strapped to the turtle's belly. The quiescent creature floated on his shell, feet crossed, arms behind his head. He wore a jaunty sailor hat and a pair of huge sunglasses. "I can't remember how many," she said. "They're all there on those shelves. Maybe someday I'll count them."

He smiled at her cavalier attitude toward her own accomplishments. Clearly, she wasn't as impressed by her talent as he was. He ran his hand and his gaze along the rows of skinny books, fat books, tall ones and tiny ones. There was a stack, lying flat, of the same kind of fabric books as the one Betsy had, but none of these was chewed.

He watched Elaina as she became deeply absorbed in her work again, wondering why she was dedicating her life to drawing pictures for other people's babies, instead of having her own. Not that she should give up her career if she had a family. He didn't think that should be required of a woman any more than it should be required of a man, and something told him Elaina McIvor was one of those people who could do and excel at both raising children and maintaining a career. If he were the one to father her children, he'd make sure that she had the time and the opportunity to continue with what she did so well.

He pulled himself up short. He had no intention of fathering any children, at any time, ever, so he'd just better keep his mind on what was important to him. And Elaina McIvor was not going to be allowed to become important.

Still, he couldn't help remembering that bag of lingerie Betsy had discovered behind a chair in the living room. He'd opened it, thinking it was more baby clothes that had somehow got missed, and had pulled out a rainbow of softness. It had created such evocative images in his mind, he had hardly dared stand up when Elaina had invited him and Betsy into her studio.

That nightgown . . . Lord, what a nightgown that was! He couldn't keep his mind off it. Sheer, it would let those rosy-red nipples of hers show through, let a man see what was happening to them long before he slowly stretched the elastic at its top and slid it down over her body. And the teddies . . . There were two of them, one black, one a slightly deeper shade of pink than the nightgown. The black one would hide everything but shape. He swallowed hard. The pink one, like the nightie, would reveal. How much? Whew! Enough! There had been panties in that bag, tiny, colorful bikini panties, and bras. Two white satin ones, a pale blue one, and a lacy black one, the latter two fastening in front.

He pictured himself sliding one hand up the satin smoothness of her stomach, fingers splayed, finding that neat little fastening and releasing it. Her breasts would leap out of confinement into his hands, his mouth, and . . .

"Brad? Is something wrong?"

Her voice startled him and he blinked her into focus. "What?" he croaked.

"What's the matter? You groaned. Don't you feel well?"

He swallowed a time or two, half in his fantasy, half out of it, not knowing which way to go. He crossed his legs and leaned forward in the big basket chair where he was seated. "I'm . . . fine," he said. "I was just . . . thinking. I'm sorry I disturbed you. Go back to work."

Elaina stared at him for another minute or two. He didn't look sick. Actually, he looked pretty good. His green eyes were shining and there was a healthy glow on his high cheekbones. He looked . . . sexy. It took her several minutes again to forget his presence and let her work take her out of herself.

When he called her for dinner, she was amazed, not only that she hadn't noticed him and Betsy leaving her studio, but that he was capable of what he had done. He had fed Betsy, she learned. Then he had somehow transformed those plebeian chicken breasts into a gourmet feast with crisp, colorful stir-fried vegetables, aromatic with sesame oil and crunchy with peanuts, and served with fluffy steamed rice.

"You can cook!"

He lifted one brow. "Of course I can." He dug into the food and ate with great concentration and little conversation, as if suddenly wondering why he was there and wanting only to finish and get out.

After they had both cleaned the kitchen and tucked the baby into her crib, he said, "I'll be back," and left.

Elaina stood and watched him drive away, feeling bereft. The evening hadn't turned out the way she had thought it might. She had pictured the two of them sitting comfortably and long over coffee once Betsy was in bed, talking, exchanging confidences, getting to know each other. Of course, she had been given no reason to anticipate such an evening. His saying that he didn't want to think about the hospital for six hours and fifty-three minutes didn't mean that he had intended to spend those hours and minutes in her company. Once Betsy was in bed, there was no further reason for him to stay.

And his kisses had simply been experimental. It seemed, she thought, that the experiment had failed. She sighed and returned to her drawing board. There she didn't have to think about a sexy green-eyed man who left her with her nerve endings all alert and calling out and her insides in a terrible turmoil.

She didn't have to think about him. But she did.

Six

Brad rang the bell and waited, scarcely aware of the sleepy sound of birds just waking up in the trees that lined Elaina's street. He wasn't even sure of how he had gotten there in the first place, but there he was. Sleep had been impossible after his horrendous night, so he had started to walk. Somehow, his feet had found their way here, and for reasons he didn't want to think about right now he had rung her bell. He heard her coming, heard her muttering something, then she swung open the door and he could only stare at her, wordless.

Her hair was a soft toast-colored tangle around her flushed face and her eyes were full of sleep, soft and luminous and slightly alarmed. She lifted a hand and brushed a leaf off his shoulder, a fleeting touch he might have imagined, but the warmth of it lingered.

"Brad?" Her voice was husky with sleep. "What's wrong?"

To his horror, he felt his eyes burn and his throat ache, and he reached out to draw her against him, burying his face against her perfumed hair. Her arms came around him and she rocked him back and forth, saying nothing, but giving comfort. He yearned to tell her all that had gone wrong, but knew if he tried to speak his voice would break.

The scent of her, the warmth, the softness of her body were like finding heaven in the most unexpected place at the most unexpected time, and he wanted to stay like this forever. Suddenly, incredibly, the ache was gone from his throat and the world lifted off his back. He sighed heavily as his mouth curved into a big, stupid smile, and he realized why his feet had brought him here. He had needed to see Elaina McIvor's luminous gray eyes, her pink mouth and her tumbled hair. He had needed to hold her, needed to breathe in her sweet scent.

His arms tightened around her. He was surprised at the intensity of his need to kiss her. He wanted to. He longed to. His heart pounded heavily in his chest. His loins tightened. What would she think of a man she hardly knew coming into her house and kissing her before she even had a chance to wake up and brush her teeth? She'd hate it! And him. And what did she think of a man she hardly knew coming into her house and grabbing her like this? He pulled himself up short and pushed her out of his arms while his gaze did the traveling his hands and mouth yearned to do.

Elaina stood rigidly, hoping her knees would hold her up. What was he doing here? Why was he looking at her like that? Hungrily, as if he were about to take her into his arms again. Not to be comforted, but to kiss her as he had yesterday . . . and as he hadn't. She was mesmerized by the gleam in the depths of his eyes. What was he thinking? What was he feeling? What was he here for?

It wasn't to kiss her, that was for sure! His gaze swept over her navy wool housecoat, contemptuously, she decided. And why not? She must look awful! He probably saw her as ugly, frumpish! Was she crazy, thinking even for a minute that he might want to kiss her and hold her and . . .

"Hi," he said, proferring a bag with grease spots decorating its outside. "I brought breakfast."

Breakfast? Bright color suffused her face. She felt the heat of it and stumbled away in a haze of embarrassment. Breakfast? That was why he'd come? She didn't want breakfast. She wanted . . . She *was* crazy! She should tell him to get lost. Breakfast!

She shut the bathroom door firmly, turned on the shower, and stripped off her bathrobe. She looked down at herself in her sexy, sheer nightie, the one he hadn't even noticed because she had covered it up in her good, decent way with her good, decent housecoat that was meant to hide things like sexy nighties and puckered nipples and shaking legs. She pulled that sexy nightie off and stuffed it deep into the hamper, feeling foolish for having worn it, foolish for having bought it, and foolish for having thought about him when she'd put it on for the first time last night.

She hadn't felt foolish then. She had felt deliciously sinful and slightly defiant and incredibly sexy, and had gone to sleep with the memory of Brad Bradshaw's lips on hers the very last thing on her mind. That must be why she had thought he wanted to kiss her just now. She was still caught up in the dreams that had filled her night. But he could know nothing of her dreams. Just as he knew nothing of her nightgown.

She was wrong. Brad had noticed the hem of peachy lace hanging below the bottom of her tailored navy bathrobe and had grinned at the contrast as she walked away. That awful robe went more with the plain white cotton pajamas and the utilitarian underwear he had found in the dryer yesterday along with Betsy's stuff. Those garments looked as if they belonged in a nunnery, but that nightgown peeking out from beneath her housecoat had come out of that hidden bag in the living room. He remembered the color. Yet somehow he knew that what he had found in the dryer was more in keeping with the facade she presented to the world.

What kind of secret fantasies did she have, he wondered, that she'd bought those delicate, lacy things, so different from her plain white cottons, built for comfort and durability, not for seduction? Were there two Elaina McIvors? The Monday Elaina who was all white cotton and practicality, and the Tuesday one, all pink lace and warm skin and sultry eyes?

What a creature of contrasts she was, he thought as he made himself at home in her kitchen, brewing coffee and setting out the doughnuts on a plate. He spent several minutes delving into those contrasts, contemplating possible reasons for them, wondering what motivated her, and why she blushed so charmingly for what seemed to him to be no good reason at all. Was she a virgin? He didn't think so. For one thing, she was too old. It simply wasn't possible that a woman could live for twenty-odd years, maybe even thirty, and remain a virgin. Not today. Her swift and potent response to his kisses told him otherwise as well.

He tried not to dwell on the surge of desire he had felt this morning, to say nothing of yesterday. He wasn't interested in her on a personal level, he told himself. It was purely clinical. He might intend to specialize in emergency medicine, but he had always had a deep interest in the workings of the human psyche. That was why Elaina fascinated him.

"Bull!" he snorted softly. Who was he trying to kid? The woman got to him on the most basic level possible. But he was simply going to have to ignore that side of things. He didn't have the time for a personal relationship, no matter how much Elaina appealed to his body. Hell, there were hundreds of women who could take care of those needs. His trouble was that he hadn't had one for far too long. He had been too busy, too tired. When the thought crossed his mind that he was still busy, still tired, and still having feelings like that about Elaina McIvor, he pushed it away. Some things didn't bear thinking about too deeply.

Half the doughnuts and two cups of coffee were gone before she came out of the bathroom, her hair damp and in little ringlets around her face. He stood up as she entered, mouth open to speak, but shut it when he discovered he didn't have any words in it. Or in his brain. She was wearing the same navy pants as yesterday, but this time they were teamed with a bright blue knit top that outlined her shapely breasts and narrow waist and tinted her gray eyes with lighter shades. And oh, lordy, those long, long legs . . .

He felt his body react to the sight of her and sat down again quickly, hiding himself behind the table.

"Do you know that it's only half past five?" she asked, pouring herself a cup of coffee and slumping into a chair across from him.

"I know," he said. "But I have to sleep today and I'm on duty again tonight, so I wouldn't be able to see . . . Betsy if I didn't come now."

"Uh-huh. And what makes you think you're going to get to see her now? If you think I want her awake at this hour of the day, think again."

"I could just look in on her, couldn't I?" he asked. "I mean, so I can tell Margo, if she regains consciousness, that I saw Betsy and she's okay?"

"I guess you could do that."

Elaina picked up one of the doughnuts and bit into it. It was so fresh and soft and yeasty that she chewed and swallowed quickly to make room in her mouth for more. It was delicious.

"I've never in my life had a doughnut for breakfast," she said when she was able to speak. Her fingers were sticky and she licked them like a child.

"How come?" He smiled at her enthusiasm and pushed the plate closer to her.

She took another one, bit, chewed, and swallowed before she shrugged one shoulder and said, "My parents are cooked-cereal-and-fresh-fruit people, with bacon and eggs for Sunday."

"No pancakes? No waffles?"

"No. I didn't have those until after I got m—away from home." She bit her lip in chagrin at her slip of the tongue. She didn't talk about Kirk and that part of her life. She had come to Eugene to forget it, had come here where no one could possibly know about Kirk and ask questions for which she had no answer. She hated for people to think she'd been stupid and naive, even though that was what she had been. For all she knew, it was what she might still be.

Brad looked hard at her. She had been going to say married. He knew that as though the word had been outlined in neon between them. Funny, but he hadn't pegged her as having been married and divorced. Widowed? He wanted to ask, but her closed expression told him she had no intention of talking about that marriage. Was it over? On hold? What? And why was it so important for him to know?

"Were you allowed to eat junk food for breakfast?" She tossed the words quickly into the silence to forestall the questions she could see flooding his eyes.

"Doughnuts are not junk food," he protested, reluctantly allowing her her privacy. There'd be other times. Later, another day, he would question her. But for now, it was easier to go with the flow and let this desultory conversation take its natural course.

Elaina watched as he took another doughnut

and bit into it, his teeth large and square and very white in his tanned face. His lips were glazed with sugar. He licked them, his gaze on her face. She licked her own lips, suddenly very much aware of him again as a man. That made her greatly aware of herself as a woman, aware of a deep pulsing sensation she wished would go away, but there didn't seem to be a lot she could do about it. He was watching her, staring at her lips, and something lurched inside her. She looked down at the table, then up again, and found his gaze still on her.

If this conversation was supposed to be taking its natural course, Brad thought desperately, then its natural course must be right into the ground. It had come upon a dam and was blocked, while words he could not speak and feelings he could not fathom built higher and higher behind it.

He cleared his throat and drank some coffee, then looked at her over the rim of his mug. "So how was she? Betsy. Last night."

"Okay. She slept well. I haven't heard a sound out of her since we put her to bed. She was uncovered when I checked on her. I covered her up."

"Good."

He didn't seem to have anything else to say. He only looked at her. The throbbing silence went on and on until all Elaina could hear was a soft, rushing roar in her ears, like a river that was about to burst its banks.

"Lainie . . ."

"Brad . . ."

He swallowed. He felt and heard his Adam's apple bobbing up and down in his throat. He pushed his chair back and stood, knowing full well that if she were to drop her eyes from his, to look down his body, she would know exactly in what way and how much she afffected him. It was suddenly important that she not know, that she not have that kind of power over him. "I've got to get out of here," he said.

She nodded, picked up their coffee mugs, and took them to the sink. He followed her with the doughnut plate, standing behind her until she turned. He saw that her hands were unsteady and wanted to clasp them in his own and tell her that what was happening to them was all right. But it wasn't all right. It was insane.

She tilted her head back to look up at him. It was a novel experience, she thought. She could look most men straight in the eye, and many she had to look down to. "Yes, you do have to go," she said, hearing the regret in her voice. "You have to sleep."

He lifted one hand and ran the back of it over her cheek. "I know." He didn't move.

"Is it quiet? Where you sleep in the hospital?" Her voice was hushed, as if she were afraid to wake someone—or something.

"Pretty quiet. I hear traffic sometimes. Ambulances. Cop cars."

"Oh."

"Is it quiet . . . here?"

"Most of the time."

They looked at each other. They both knew that what they were thinking was impossible. Impractical. Betsy could cry. The little boys next door could—and would—ring the bell. And he had a perfectly good bed waiting for him in his own quarters. There was no need. Still . . .

He stroked her cheek one more time and stepped away. She walked with him to the door.

Again, she thought he might kiss her, but he turned after a moment and loped out to the gate. He looked over his shoulder at her, opened the gate, and walked out. She closed the door and leaned on it, feeling more empty and alone than she'd ever felt before.

When the door was forcefully thrust open, it carried her with it. He caught her as she stumbled, trying to regain her balance.

"I forgot something," he said, and pulled her tightly against him, letting her feel his hard arousal. He bent to take her lips in a brief, potent kiss that left her lungs gasping, her head spinning, and her body humming, clamoring for more.

But he didn't give her more, even when her arms twined around his neck and her lips clung to his. He set her away from him and said, "Smile, Lainie. I want to go to sleep thinking of your smile." She smiled and he added softly, "I'll be back."

It wasn't until her heart had finally settled down, her head had stopped spinning, and her smile had faded that she realized he had forgotten to look in on Betsy before he left.

A couple of days later, they were cleaning the kitchen after a shared lunch. Betsy was tucked into bed for a nap and Brad had half an hour before he needed to be back at the hospital. As she washed, he wiped down the counters. That was just one of the things Elaina was learning to like about him. He didn't sit around, as Kirk had, and expect to be waited on. He also took over most of Betsy's care when he was here, giving Elaina the much needed time to complete her assignment. Of course, that was why he came, she reminded herself. To see Betsy. There had been no kisses today, none yesterday or the day before, and no long looks or gentle caresses that suggested he might have kissing on his mind—or anything more.

"What brought you to Oregon?" she asked. She had wondered a lot about that, among other things. He had told her about his big, closely-knit family—his parents and several of his four brothers and sisters were in Buffalo, yet he lived here, thousands of miles away.

"I live here because this is where my wife was from," he answered. "When I got out of the army, she wanted to come back here." He shrugged and rinsed the dishcloth, then wrung it out and hung it neatly over the small rail inside the cupboard door under the sink. "But when she realized it wasn't military life she had disliked but marriage to me, I was already partway through medical school here and didn't care to leave. We divorced and she moved to San Francisco where there's some action. That's what she said she wanted."

"I'm sorry," Elaina said. She'd had no idea he'd been married. "Do you have children?"

"No. We planned to wait until after I finished the tour I was on when we got married. I'd just re-enlisted for five years and that seemed like a pretty nice honeymoon period. Only when the tour was over, so was the honeymoon and the marriage."

"Do you miss her?"

He smiled and shook his head. "It's been nearly four years, Lainie." He moved closer, grasped her chin, and tilted her face up. Before she could react, he placed a firm, warm kiss on her lips, but not the kiss she had longed for. "You look so worried," he said, as if he needed to provide a reason for having kissed her. "You care more about people than you like to pretend, Elaina."

"I've never pretended I don't care about people," she protested. She wondered bleakly if he suspected just how deeply she was beginning to care about him. Maybe that was why he had avoided kissing her until just now, and why the kiss had been too close to brotherly for comfort.

"You don't care much—or say you don't—about your own family," he reminded her.

She had no argument for that. It was true. He'd been shocked to learn of the infrequency of her family's letters.

"Everybody needs to feel loved," Brad had told her, "to feel part of a greater unit. I'm the oldest of five children and I feel close to my brothers and sisters and to my mom, too. My baby sister is in school in New Mexico, and I'm in close touch with her." He paused. "Have you ever been in love?" She knew he was hinting for her to tell him about Kirk, but she still resisted that with all her might. She wondered now if it had been her need to feel loved that had made her so vulnerable to Kirk, if that was why she had responded to her belief—erroneous, she knew now—that he loved her. She had fallen for him like the very young fool she had been.

And wasn't she in danger of doing the same with Brad? Did she have to respond to any kind of affection, no matter how casual, so wholeheartedly? She sighed and stepped away from him, moving to the far side of the kitchen, putting space between them. He followed her. She opened the door and fled into the backyard. He caught her shoulders and turned her to face him before letting her go. He wasn't touching her, not quite. But still he kept her from escaping the intensity of his gaze.

"Are you running away from me, Elaina?"

"Of course not. I just want to be outside. It's a nice day."

He smiled a soft, warm smile that made her toes curl up. "Fibber. Don't play games with me, Lainie. Okay?"

Held by the magnetism of his green eyes, she whispered, "I'm not." Then, needing to remind him as well as herself of his reason for being there, she asked, "How do you know so much about taking care of babies?"

"Nieces and nephews," he said and grinned. "I love taking care of them whenever they visit me or I get back home to visit them."

She shifted uneasily. "How's Margo?" she asked.

His smile faded. "There's no real change in her condition."

"Poor Margo," she said, meaning "poor Brad." She was nearly overcome by the urge to take him in her arms, to hold him and comfort him as she had the other morning.

Why had she done so? That was another thing she had wondered about. It had been an impulse, and she wasn't normally a person to give in to impulses. But he cared so much! That made her care all the more about him, and she must not. Again she moved away from him. She snapped a dead rose from a stem and dropped it to the rich soil beneath the bush.

He plucked a bud and tucked it behind her ear. For a moment he looked at her, then he strode away along the paved path at the side of the house. She heard the rough sound of his van starting up and realized that this time he hadn't said he'd be back. Maybe now he knew it went without saying. But he hadn't kissed her, either, and she felt deprived.

"Stroke! Stroke! Stro—Dammit, Bradshaw, get your mind on what you're doing! Are you rowing or chopping wood?"

"Sorry, cox," Brad muttered. The coxswain was right. He wasn't concentrating as he should be. He wasn't forgetting the agony he had dealt with all night and letting the steady, rhythmic motion, the dip and pull and lean and stretch of muscles soothe him as it was supposed to. He forced himself to focus on the rhythm of rowing, to work with the rest of the crew, to send the scull skimming over the calm, early-morning surface of the lake, to zero in on the inner self that drove the boat along, to concentrate on rowing with the same intensity as Lainie did on drawing.

He pictured her perched on her high stool at

her board, eyes dark and deep as she worked. He got so much pleasure out of watching her work. It was strange, the delight she gave him during those hours when he sat there, simply watching her . . .

Lainie . . . He wished he could control what was happening to him where she was concerned. Ever since he had gone there that morning—at five-thirty, for Pete's sake—woken her up, had breakfast with her and tried to pretend that he'd come to see Betsy, he'd known there was something afoot that he couldn't get a handle on. Of course he hadn't expected the baby to be awake. Nor had he wanted her to be. He had wanted exactly what he had gotten—an hour of Elaina's company. Even though he hadn't told her any of the horrible things he had seen, it was as if he had unburdened himself to her. When he left her, he felt renewed and strengthened and ready to sleep, so that he was able to go back on duty that next night and do it all over again.

That was where he wanted to be now, he thought, talking to her, looking at her, absorbing the calm of her gray eyes, calmer even than this fog-silvered lake, instilling peace in his soul. She had such inner serenity. She was very much all together. If he were ever to marry again, it would have to be to someone like Elaina. Not that he was going to marry again. But if—

"Bradshaw? Are you with us, or agin us?"

"Oh, hell! Sorry, cox."

He should have turned up on duty fully refreshed after his morning workout on the lake, but he didn't, and the day was long, tiresome, and tiring. He didn't begin to feel good until he found himself where he wanted to be, sitting in Elaina's studio in the evening, telling her about his day. In the telling, the horror of it washed away and he felt as clean and complete as if it had never happened.

"Lord, forgive me, Lainie," he said. He reached over to the wicker couch where she was sitting and took her hand, stroking her long, supple fingers. "Why do you let me dump on you that way?"

She smiled. "I don't mind. Your day is more interesting than mine."

She squeezed his hand before pulling loose from him. He frowned. The past few days she had been doing that a lot, pulling away from him. He'd thought they were past her nervousness over being touched. He wished he knew what was going on in her head. She listened whenever he wanted to talk, patient, interested, sympathetic, but what was she getting out of their relationship? It seemed to him that all he did was waste her time.

"But we came in here so you could work," he said contritely. "Don't you want to? I wish you would. I like watching you draw."

"I not only want to, I have to. Deadline is approaching closer and closer." She walked over to her drawing board and hitched herself onto the high stool.

"When do you go into practice on your own?" she asked, uncapping inks and putting nibs on pens. She glanced over at him as he sat slumped in what had become his favorite chair, legs extended far out in front, ankles crossed on the padded wicker stool.

"I could have done that a few months ago," he

said. "But I took another year's residency in the E.R. I plan to specialize in emergency medicine. It's a relatively new field and there's something about it that appeals to me."

"Yet it bothers you so much," she said, frowning at him over the top of her table. "I've been wondering why you stay with it. Isn't there something else you could do that wouldn't be so—so stressful?"

He shrugged. "I don't know. It's a high. I love it and I hate it. It's like living on the edge all the time. The alarm goes and you know an ambulance is on its way in. You don't know what it will bring, but the adrenaline starts pumping and the mind goes into high gear. It . . . well, I can't possibly explain it, but it gets to me, it fulfills me, gives me something that I've only experienced in a rowing match."

She nodded encouragingly and he went on.

"It's a constant competition and the opponent is death. And even while I hate it, I feed on it.

"Other doctors in emergency medicine feel the same. And the nurses. But the burnout rate is high, really high. And it makes for lousy family life. Two of my colleagues had to get out of it because of what it was doing to their families—and to their own health. It's wild, knowing that if we don't work fast and accurately and expertly, lives can be lost. There's an ego trip in having to be right all the time. There are no moments to pause and reflect and decide at your leisure what course of treatment to take. It's a *now* kind of medicine. And it takes all a doctor's emotions and attention and strength."

She had seen him totally depleted often enough to know he was right. He was probably right, too, in his assessment of what that kind of work must do to a marriage. The thought left her feeling low and melancholy, and she escaped those forbidden thoughts by immersing herself totally in her drawing.

She didn't know how much time had passed when she became aware of Brad standing behind her. Lifting her head, she rubbed her stiff neck. He brushed her hand aside, taking over the job himself.

She sighed in pleasure as his strong fingers worked over her aching neck and shoulders. "Ummm . . . that feels good," she murmured. She let him lean her head back against his chest as he began to massage her upper arms and the front muscles of her shoulders. The heat of his body burned into her back and she shifted her head, a soft moan rising in her throat as his fingers slid down over the upper curves of her breasts. She drew in a shaky breath and turned her face toward his neck.

He slipped one hand under her chin, tilting her face up, looking into her eyes. Her heart slammed against her ribs. She knew he was going to kiss her, could feel it in the possessive curve of his hand around her chin. His other hand caught her shoulder as he stepped back and turned her so that she faced him. He parted her knees and stood between them, holding her loosely with one arm. The other hand moved, one finger outlining her ear before he slid into the softness of her hair.

"Sweet Lainie," he said. "Sweet, sweet Lainie. I

should run like hell, shouldn't I? But all I want to do is kiss you."

"Yes," she said. She didn't want to run anymore either.

"Yes, what?" His smile hovered just above her lips. "Yes, I should run, or yes, I should kiss you?"

She laid her hand flat on his chest, feeling the warmth of him through his shirt, feeling the soft, curling hairs beneath the cloth. She ached to run her fingers through it. Instead, she slipped her arms around him.

His lips brushed over hers, not kissing, just asking again. "Well?"

He had never asked permission before. He was asking about more than a kiss. She drew in a deep breath. It was filled with his scent and made her dizzy. "I understand that running, if you're not used to it, can cause heart attacks." She didn't think this man ever ran from a woman. He might have to fight them off with a baseball bat at times, but he never turned and ran.

"That's true," he said solemnly. "A proven medical fact." He brushed his lips across hers again and she felt herself melting, felt her fingers flex as they clung to his back, then slid down and caught on his belt, holding on so she wouldn't fall. Her stool was a frail, precarious perch in the storm that was beginning to blow around her.

"Better not take any unnecessary risks," she murmured, and he nodded just before he covered her lips with his own.

Seven

From the very beginning it wasn't an ordinary kiss. The moment his lips touched hers, they burned and something zingingly electric stung her nerves, jerking her closer to him. When the probing tip of his tongue touched her lower lip, she shivered with a delicious sensation and opened her mouth to welcome it. Moaning softly, he tilted her head and plunged deeply inside her, drinking from her as if he were parched. His arms locked around her and she pressed closer to him, reveling in the hardness of his thighs as he crowded in closer between hers, loving the way her body yielded to his until they seemed molded together. Her breasts flattened against him, hard peaks jutting forth to press into the wall of his chest.

He lifted his head long enough to look into her eyes and say, "Elaina . . ." in a tone of wonder and delight. "I've wanted to kiss you like that since the first time I held you." And then he was kissing her again, moving his hands over her body, down her back, cupping her buttocks. He pulled her off the stool and stepped away from it with her still wrapped around him, moving her sensuously against him until she moaned and buried her hands in his thick crisp hair.

It tingled on her palms, made her fingers curl, and she traced the shape of his skull with her hands. Pressing herself ever more tightly to him, she pulled his head down until his mouth was fused with hers, their tongues dueling, meshing, parting, then coming back to stroke and caress. He rocked her body slowly against his hardness as he moved his lips over her cheek, down her throat, pausing to press his tongue against the wild pulse that beat there, and then down to the high neck of her blouse. He stopped and returned his lips to hers, setting her back onto her stool while he attacked the barrier he had found.

His fingers shook as he undid the narrow strings that tied in a bow around her neck. He fumbled with the buttons and undid two of them, his breath hot and moist as it met her skin. She arched up, a soft, throaty sound of pleasure emanating from her as he kissed her, parting more buttons and finally finding her breast.

She felt a moment's regret that she wasn't wearing one of her lovely new bras, or a sheer teddy, but when his thumb rubbed over her nipple, squeezing it, pulling it with a gentle, seductive tugging that sent messages of urgency throughout her body, she forgot everything but his touch and the hunger it aroused in her.

"Please," she whispered. "Please . . ."

He slipped her breast free and took the nipple into his mouth, drawing it in deep. The hot wetness of his tongue scalded her, making her gasp and clutch at his head.

How she had yearned for this, heart and soul and body. She felt like a woman for the first time in years. She wanted him. Needed him to make her complete. Her blood sang, her muscles quivered, and she felt herself growing lighter and lighter, floating away. But she wasn't. He was lifting her and carrying her to the wicker couch. She felt the heat of his body as it pressed against her, his weight the only thing preventing her from sailing away, and she held him, tighter and tighter.

He tangled his hands in her hair, holding her head still while he plundered her mouth, then his lips left hers and his fingers traced her face, her throat, her upper chest and shoulders. He slid away from her, took off her blouse and her bra, then laid her back, kneeling beside the couch and gazing at her as if he found her beautiful.

Slowly, he reached out and cupped one breast, brushing his thumb back and forth under the nipple until it strained upward in anticipation. She gasped and clasped her hands behind his head, pulling it down, placing his mouth over her nipple.

"Ah, Lainie . . . you taste so sweet," he said, and sucked hard on her. Her back arched as she curled her fingers around his head, responding to the deep pull of sensation his mouth on her evoked.

She managed to insert a hand in between them and fumbled with the buttons on his shirt. At last her hand could rest on his bare chest, and her palm circled across it, finding one of his nipples. She squeezed it to the same rhythm of his sucking and heard him moan. He moved his hand down over her flat belly and curved it between her thighs. He pressed against her, making soft, insinuating circles, his fingers squeezing gently into her softness, and she lifted one knee to make it easier for him to caress her.

He undid the snap at her waist, slid down the zipper, and reached inside to discover the softness of her skin, the lushness of the golden-brown hair barely covered by her bikini panties.

"Brad!" He didn't know if her soft gasp was in protest or delight, and lifted his head. Her eyes were tightly closed, her lips parted and moist, and her breasts, one shiny and wet from his mouth, heaving from the force of her breathing.

"Lainie . . ." he murmured, his hand still making gentle circles on her body. She opened her eyes, and her gaze was all hot smoke and desire. Once more, he cupped her chin and jaw, rubbing a thumb over her lips. "I want to make love to you."

Her body tingling, she knew that if he didn't make love to her, she would go mad with need. Oh, Lord, how she wanted him!

"Brad . . ." His name seemed to be all she was capable of saying. "Brad . . ."

The piping skirl of his beeper cut into whatever she might have been going to say. He cursed as he dropped his head to her bare abdomen, his breathing ragged and pained.

"No!" he raged. "Oh, God, no, not *now*!"

But the beeper went on and on.

He lifted his head and stared at the box on his belt as if it were an alien spacecraft.

"Don't answer it," she cried.

He transferred his alien-spacecraft stare to her and she groaned. "I'm sorry. That was stupid. You have to, don't you?"

"I have to," he said raggedly. He shut off the insistent sound of the beeper and stroked her hair back from her forehead. "Do you know how badly I want to ignore it?"

She nodded, then turned her face and kissed his palm.

He jerked away from her. "Don't!" he said, then laughed roughly. "God! You make me crazy, Elaina McIvor. Do you know that? When I'm near you, everything that matters goes skittering away and all I want to do is hold you and kiss you and make love to you forever and ever. Do you always have that effect on men?"

But even as he was saying it, he was buttoning his shirt, tucking it in, striding across the room.

She sat up and pulled her blouse back on, watching as he dialed the number of the emergency room. He spoke briefly, gave a couple of terse instructions, then said, "On my way."

She walked him to the door, her hand linked in his, but instead of kissing her as she had expected, he only squeezed her fingers before drawing them to his cheek. He held them against his face for a moment, his eyes dark and unreadable, then said, "Yup. That's it. Crazy. Totally, completely out of my mind. It's got to stop, Elaina. It's got to stop now."

And then he left.

After four days she concluded that once back in the familiar environment of broken bodies, gushing blood, and screaming sirens, he had rediscovered sanity, and found he preferred it.

Finally, he phoned on Sunday afternoon to say that Margo had regained consciousness and was asking about Betsy. Could Elaina, he asked, write Margo a short note telling her about the baby? He thought it would be beneficial.

His voice was brisk and cool and impersonal, and Elaina scolded herself for caring. She should have known all along that what had happened between them wasn't something he wanted. Not really. Oh, he had wanted to make love to her then, at that moment, but once away from her, he knew what he wanted more. The excitement of emergency medicine. How could she compete?

"Of course I'll write her a note," she said, her tone as cool as his. "What's the address of the hospital, and her room number?"

He didn't offer to come and get the note. He just gave her the necessary information.

Elaina wrote the note, and more. She made sketches. Every day, new sketches and another note. She got no replies, but that didn't matter. She filmed Betsy with her video camera—in the bath, in her high chair covered with chocolate pudding, playing with the two little boys next door who had forgiven her for being a girl-baby. Someday she could show Margo the videos. In the meantime, they were there for her files, all those moods and poses and expressions, ready to use when she needed inspiration for illustrations—once Betsy was gone.

She kept herself busy. She worked whenever she could, played with Betsy, had coffee several times with Terri next door, and tried not to think about Brad. But she missed him. Lord, how she missed him. A hundred times a day she thought of excuses to call him, but none of them was valid. He would see through them. He would see through her. He would laugh at her. She couldn't bear that. So strongly did she resist the idea of calling him that when Betsy got sick and she had a real, legitimate excuse to call, she still hesitated. But Betsy cried, and cried. Her skin was hot and dry and flushed, and not one of those many books Elaina had bought offered a concrete explanation. As far as she could make out, it could be anything from temper to meningitis.

She had to call.

"Not there?" she asked the woman who answered. Once before, she remembered, she had called and he hadn't been there. But then, he hadn't been there because he had been here. "Where is he? The baby's sick! She needs him. I need him," she admitted, fighting tears. "He has a beeper. Can't you page him?"

"I'm sorry, no. He's off duty. He's out of the hospital." That never seemed to matter when he was with her, did it? They beeped him whenever they chose, interrupting whatever might be going on. But now, tonight, when she needed to have him paged, would they beep him? Of course not!

"You'll have to call your own doctor or bring the baby in here," said the disembodied, uncaring voice. "How high is her temperature?"

Elaina didn't know the answer to that and hung up, feeling desperate and abandoned. She paced with Betsy, debating wrapping her up and doing as the voice had suggested, taking her to the hospital. She was on the verge of doing so when the doorbell rang.

She flew to the door, flung it open, then burst into tears when she saw it was only Terri Greenspan standing there.

"Hi," Terri said. "Do you need help? That baby's been crying for nearly half an hour. You must need a break. Teething's a terrible time, isn't it?"

How easy it all seemed after that. Terri rubbed some numbing gel on Betsy's swollen gums and dripped liquid aspirin onto her tongue, and within minutes the baby was sleeping quietly. Exhausted, Elaina curled up on the spare bed in case she was needed, and fell into a deep sleep.

When the doorbell screeched at a few minutes past daybreak, Elaina jerked awake, but the baby slept on. Muttering, grumbling, cussing under her breath about weird doctors who worked strange hours and came calling at even stranger ones, she stuffed her arms into the sleeves of her bathrobe and tied it as she ran. She tried to smooth her hair, wishing she had time to brush her teeth, and wondered if she looked all sleep-wrinkled and puffy-eyed. Then she berated herself for caring. He was coming to see Betsy, not her, but at last he was here again and she couldn't control the hammering of her heart.

As the bell sounded once more, she unlocked the door, wrenched it open, and stared up at a stretch of pale blue sky with no dark head or laughing green eyes anywhere up there at all. She looked down, and down, and met the tear-filled brown eyes of a half-naked five-year-old who was standing there with a handful of wilted dandelions.

"I got lock-ed out," he said. "Can I come in? My feet are cold."

"Petey!" she said, recognizing the younger of Terri's two boys. "Oh, my goodness. Yes. Come in. Did you ring the bell at home? Didn't your parents hear you?" She could see he was cold all over, and shivering. He was wearing only a T-shirt with a picture of a bulldog on it and a pair of the most ridiculously tiny jockey shorts.

"Petey," she asked, shutting the door behind him, "why didn't you ask your mom and dad to let you in? Or your brother?"

He ambled into her studio and curled up in the big basket chair. Quickly, she covered him with an afghan robe, tucking it in around him.

"Billy's sleepin' over at Kevin's house and Daddy's gone to work and Mommy's sleepin' in."

"Well, we better call her and tell her where you are."

"No!" Petey's eyes widened. "Daddy said he'd skin me if I woke her up. He told me to be real quiet and watch telubision until the clock on the stove said eight-oh-oh. It's her birfday and I wanted to pick her some flowers to go with the ones Daddy got her and I went outside to pick some and the door got lock-ed." He made two syllables out of the last word again.

Elaina glanced at her watch. It still lacked an hour and a half before "eight-oh-oh" and she didn't know what to do. Of course she should call Terri and let her know her youngest son had escaped but was safe. But it was her birthday, and after all the help she'd given Elaina last night, she certainly deserved a break today.

"Would you like to stay for breakfast?" she asked Petey. "I could call your mom and tell her you're here, then your dad wouldn't be mad at you for waking her up. We'll just tell her to go back to sleep and have a good rest while you and I look after each other. What do you think?"

He beamed. "Yes, please, Miss McIby."

Elaina had to grin at him. He really was cute.

"Hey," she said. "We're friends. Why don't you call me Lainie?"

She blinked. *Lainie?* Had she really said that? Yup. She really had. Shaking her head, she quickly made the call. Terri argued about her keeping Petey, but not for long. Elaina suggested she come for breakfast, too, when she woke up again.

"Now, I'm sure you won't want to wait and have breakfast with your mom and me," she said to Petey. "So tell me what you like."

"Eggs and bacon and toast and hotcakes and syrup and sausages and cereal and johnnycake," he said. "Can I have a picnic outside?"

Elaina stared at him. Eggs, toast, and cereal she could manage, but the rest of it? She studied him carefully. Nope. He didn't eat all of those things for breakfast. He was simply too small to hold that much food. "Eggs," she said. "And toast."

"Okay. Eggs to dunk and fingers. And a picnic?" he asked again hopefully.

"A picnic, sure, but it's still cold out. The sun won't be on the patio for another hour. You'll need a sweater."

He giggled to see himself dressed in one of her pullovers. It came down almost to his ankles, and the long socks she pulled onto him were nearly hidden. She rolled up the sleeves of the sweater and left him sitting happily at the patio table waiting for his breakfast. She put on the coffee, washed her face and tied her hair back before rushing into the kitchen to get Petey's breakfast ready before Betsy woke up and demanded hers.

This was rather fun, she thought, rushing around to get one child settled with what he needed before the other one woke up, just like a real mother. It gave her a feeling of efficiency, of competence, to know how well she was coping. She wished, just for a second or two, that Kirk could see her now, cooking scrambled eggs for the one child sitting on the patio waiting for her, while the baby was still sleeping peacefully after a bad night. Sleeping because Elaina had looked after her, made her better, comforted her when she was in pain. That Terri had been the one to do all that was beside the point. Now that Elaina knew how, she would be able to do the same. Kirk had been so wrong! She would make a good mother.

Well, maybe she had a long way to go, she thought a few minutes later. But no one learned everything overnight.

Petey glowered at her mutinously, eyes filling with tears, lower lip jutting. He wanted eggs to dunk and fingers, and she had given him mucky eggs. He was going home!

He hesitated when she reminded him that his mother was sleeping because it was her birthday. He stopped when she mentioned that his daddy might skin him.

While she was trying to be patient and reason with him, Betsy woke up, screaming. She had to leave Petey with the breakfast he hated to take care of Betsy. She changed the baby, dressed her as quickly as possible, and got bitten by a couple of sharp little teeth when she tried to rub more gel on Betsy's gums. Then, rushing into the kitchen with her, she stepped on Harrison's tail. He dug two paws worth of claws into her ankle, raked them through her flesh, and flew to the top of the counter. He knocked over the bottle of cooking oil whose lid she had forgotten to replace, and Petey, coming to see if she had decided to relent and provide him with eggs to dunk, slipped in the resulting slick and bumped his head. He howled.

Trying to get a bottle for Betsy, whose wails were undiminished, and comfort Petey, who was leaning on the table sobbing, and get Harrison off the counter where he was uncharacteristically eating the butter, and stop her own blood from smearing all over the floor, Elaina feared for her sanity. In the living room, the telephone began to ring, and ring, and ring. All she needed now was the doorbell, she thought, and in response it blared its ugly sound not once, but twice. Petey, feeling neglected, lay down on the floor and drummed his heels.

Into all this walked a big-footed man who stood in the doorway and said loudly, "Hey! You left the door unlocked again, you— Wow! Who the hell are you? Mother Goose? Where'd you get the other kid? At a rummage sale?"

The baby bottle was plastic. It bounced off his forehead without breaking. . . . anything.

"What did you do that for?" he asked, completely flabbergasted. He picked up the bottle. Betsy saw it and screamed louder.

"Answer the phone!" Elaina shouted.

He returned to the kitchen a minute later and yelled, "Do you want to buy a set of encyclopedias?" She stared at him, mute with disbelief.

"I didn't think so," he said. "So I told them no."

He rinsed the bottle and took Betsy from Elaina, then sat down at the table. He was near Petey who still lay on the floor, but was no longer bellowing, his tantrum having been ignored. He still sniffled and rubbed his head, staring curiously at the strange man. When Brad stuffed the nipple into Betsy's mouth and silence permitted Elaina's brain to function again, all she could think of was how glad she was to see Brad.

She removed Harrison from the counter, set the empty butter dish in the sink, and glanced at Brad again. If he was as happy to see her, there was no way of telling. He didn't even look at her.

He looked at Petey. Stared at him, really. His mouth twitched but he didn't laugh at the child's strange garb. Instead, he asked, "What's your name, pal?"

"Petermalcolmgreenspan." Petey got to his feet, his lower lip again jutting resentfully. He gave Elaina a dirty look.

Elaina didn't know how Brad managed to decipher three separate words from that muttered sound, but supposed he must have trained himself to listen closely.

"Well, then, Peter Malcolm Greenspan, what seems to be the trouble?"

"I don't like mucky eggs. I want eggs to dunk and she won't make them. And fingers." So now it was all her fault, was it? she thought. Petey seemed to have forgotten that he'd bumped his head. He looked hopefully at Brad. "Can you cook breffus?"

"Breffus," said Brad, looking at Elaina for the first time since he'd sat down. He grinned. "He probably eats pus-ketty for dinner too."

"That," she said dryly, "I could have handled. I used to eat pus-ketty myself. But eggs to dunk? What in the world would he dunk them in? And fingers? Is the kid cannibalistic?"

Brad laughed softly and the sound curled itself around her, warming her. "Try frying the eggs with the yolks soft and cutting the toast into little strips. It's the toast that gets dunked. In the egg yolks."

He turned out to be absolutely right, and Elaina set Petey back up at the table on the patio for his picnic. Brad carried Betsy, now all smiles and bubbles, and her high chair out to join him. He spooned Pablum baby cereal then apple-raspberry goop into her. Elaina sat down and finally sipped at her first cup of coffee while the sun rose over the treetops and flooded into the yard like a benediction.

Birds sang. The scent of roses filled the fresh morning air. It was a good morning to be alive, she thought. She glanced over at Brad. *I love him,* she thought. *I absolutely, utterly, and completely love the man.*

As if sensing her gaze on him, he looked up and smiled. "What's been going on here this morning?" he asked softly.

"You don't want to know. Tell me, baby expert, how in the world did you know about eggs to dunk and fingers?"

"I used to eat toast fingers myself," he said, and grinned at Petey, who was industriously dunking and munching, happily oblivious of anything but his food.

Picking up Elaina's hand, Brad drew one of her fingers into his mouth and nibbled on it. "Now I like fingers of a different kind."

A tremor ran through her and she tugged her hand out of his grasp, but not before he placed a kiss on her palm and curled her fingers in over it.

"What happened to your ankle?" he asked.

"Harrison scratched me when I stepped on him. He didn't mean to hurt me. It was just an instinctive reaction on his part."

"You better let me have a look at it." He lifted her foot to his lap, his long, strong fingers firm on her skin. He pushed back the leg of her cotton pajamas, and she could feel the heat of his gaze on her. If this went on much longer, she would melt into a puddle on her chair.

"It needs to be cleaned and bandaged," he said, his voice thick. His fingers were still caressing, sliding up her calf now, inside the leg of her pajamas.

Her pajamas! She had long since given up wearing the pink nightie. He was never going to see it. He didn't want to see it. Or did he?

He wasn't looking at her ankle but her face, and she met his gaze and drowned in it, and knew that her scratches were far, far from his mind.

"Hi, there," said a bright voice. Terri came through the gate in the high hedge, grinning at her son in his eccentric garb and pretending not to notice how quickly Elaina snatched her bare foot off the lap of the big, good-looking guy who had his hand halfway up her leg.

"Oh. Hi." Elaina stood up, her face a brilliant color. "This is Brad. Dr. Bradshaw. He was . . . um, looking at my ankle. The cat scratched me."

She poured Terri coffee with a hand that shook, waved her to a chair, and slid a plate of cantaloupe wedges close to her. "Help yourself."

"I will, I will, don't worry about me," Terri said, and turned to Brad. "How do you do?" she asked.

Brad was barely able to drag his gaze off Elaina's face long enough to return her greeting.

Terri sat down beside her son and gave Betsy back the toys she had thrown from the high chair.

"Don't let me keep medical science from working its wonders," she said. "That ankle does look like it needs attention."

"Yes," Brad said. He grabbed Elaina's hand and nearly dragged her inside.

He thrust her into the bathroom as if he really meant to treat her ankle, but as soon as the door was shut he leaned on it and stared into her eyes. "If I don't get to kiss you in less than ten seconds I am going to explode," he said rapidly. "Come here."

She went.

"What . . . have . . . you . . . done . . . to . . . me?" he asked between kisses, his eyes closed, his cheek rubbing against hers. He needed a shave. He prickled. He felt wonderful. "I have thought of you, dreamed of you, wished I was with you every waking minute and most of my sleeping ones for the past eternity since I saw you."

"Me too," she breathed, tasting the salty flavor of his neck with her lips and tongue. "You said you'd be back but you didn't come."

"I know." He didn't give her any explanation, just those two words. "I'm sorry. Did you miss me?"

"I missed you."

He untied her belt, parted her navy robe, and looked at her for a long moment. "I missed you too."

He kissed her again, deeply, searchingly, demanding a response and getting it. Straining her closer, he held her head with one hand and her buttocks with the other, moving her back and forth across the hardness of his body until she sobbed in need and dug her nails into his back. "I thought about you all the time, and I wanted to be with you, but . . . Oh, hell, Lainie, I've never been more confused in my life!" His kiss was filled with hunger and anger, though she didn't know what she had done to deserve that anger.

She took her hands from behind his head and stared into his eyes. "I don't understand, Brad. What could be confusing about me?"

He kissed her eyes shut, cradled her face in his hands, and touched her lips with his again. "You give me the most erotic dreams, and there's no rational reason for it. God, you wear pajamas!" His laugh was soft and incredulous, and he kissed her throat down to the collar of her top. "Until I met you, I didn't even know they made pajamas for women! Why do you wear them when I know perfectly well you have at least one sexy, slinky gown? And why do I have fantasies about you, not in that nightgown but just like this, in your long-legged, long-sleeved, buttoned-up-to-the-neck pajamas! And this ugly tailored robe." The robe was pushed off her and fell to the floor. "You dress like a prude, Elaina McIvor! You wear your hair like an old-maid librarian."

He gently removed the elastic band from her hair, then massaged her scalp and spread the hair over her shoulders. He drew a strand of it under her nose like a mustache, nearly making her sneeze. She reached up to move it, but he caught her wrist in his free hand. He nudged aside her sleeve as his lips slid up her arm to her elbow, his tongue pressing against the sensitive skin there before moving back down to her fingers. She curled her hand around his face and drew his mouth back up to hers. She kissed him softly, running her tongue around his lips, slipping it inside to find his, to caress it, to tempt it to follow back into the warm moistness of her mouth.

"The first time I saw you I doubted the pose," he said thickly, "because of your eyes. And your mouth. It's beautiful and warm and sensuous and it begs to be kissed even when you're holding it in a tight, firm line while you look like a proper lady. And then when I touch it with mine, all the secret promises that mouth makes are fulfilled and you come alive in my arms." His breath burned her shoulder through the cotton of her pajamas.

"You tease me and excite me even when you're dressed like a nun, because I know you'll melt and turn into a wanton, a siren, a houri, when I kiss y—"

"A *what*?" she squawked, pulling back from him. "That's an insult!"

"Houri," he said, stressing both syllables. He dragged her back against the full length of his body, parting his thighs to pull her into him. "You know. One of the pasha's most beautiful nymphs. Only nymphs don't wear crisp cotton pajamas that shouldn't be able to turn a man on at all. And still you seduce me. Oh, Elaina, lovely Lainie, seduce me some more."

He kissed her again and she saw what he meant about her coming alive in his arms. She knew they should stop, but what was happening felt too good to stop. She slipped her arms around his neck again, pulling his mouth down to her as she gave herself over to the magic they created together.

It was he who called a halt. "Enough," he said, panting. He dragged her arms from around him, holding her off and resting his forehead against hers. "No. I lie. It's not enough. I don't think I'll ever get enough of you, but we can't keep doing this or I'll never be able to walk out of here." His eyes were incredibly green, laughing into hers, and she trembled as she moved closer, telling him with her body, her eyes, what she couldn't yet say out loud. She didn't want him to walk out. Ever.

"How do you know about my sexy nightie?" she asked, then hid her blush behind her hair.

For a moment, his arms came around her again and he pressed his cheek on top of her head. She heard the small sound he made as he swallowed, then he set her back from him again, tipping her face up so he could see her eyes. His were no longer laughing.

"I saw it in the bag the day you bought it," he said huskily, "and then I saw it again the next day, peeking out from under your bathrobe." He drew in a deep breath. "Why did you buy it, Lainie? And the other stuff? Was it for me?"

She stared into his eyes for a long moment, then nodded. He touched her cheek. "Oh, Elaina. I wish . . ."

"Wish what?"

"Wish it were night, not morning. Wish we were alone. Wish I could see you with that nightie on. And off. Oh, hell, I wish things were different all around," he added, sad and disheartened.

She could only look at him, bewildered.

"Sit down," he said. "Let's see your ankle."

His eyes were serious, his mouth a straight line, and he didn't look at her as he opened the medicine cabinet.

He treated her minor wounds, and the difference between his touch now and his touch earlier was vast. His hand was still warm on her flesh, still firm, but now it was completely impersonal, totally sexless. She might have been a wax dummy, she thought. Or a patient.

When he was finished, he stood and opened the door. He gazed at her somberly for a moment but said nothing. Then he left, closing the door behind him as if placing a barrier between them.

But he hadn't had to do that, she thought bleakly. His eyes had done it first.

Eight

The sound of Brad's laughter drew Elaina to the patio and she stood in the doorway watching him playing cat's cradle with Petey, while Terri looked on. Betsy was standing holding onto Brad's knee, occasionally reaching out to touch the intricately woven strings.

Terri said something and Brad laughed again. Clearly, his morose mood hadn't lasted long. With a sigh, Elaina remembered she had invited her neighbor for breakfast, and turned to prepare it.

Petey had given her the idea: johnnycake. She quickly assembled the ingredients and mixed up the corn bread recipe she hadn't used for a long, long time. She put the pan in the oven, set the timer and returned to her studio. At the door leading out to the patio, she paused, taking in the warmth of the picture her guests made.

Terri looked up, saw her, and smiled. With a gesture that said, "Stay there, and keep quiet," Elaina turned to grab a sketch pad.

She drew them as a group first, capturing the scene that she knew her mind would hold forever. She was nearly sick with a sudden tearing of longing, with the desire for a family of her own. She had told herself for so long it was a futile dream, but was it? Why shouldn't she want—and have—the most natural thing in the world for a woman to want? She tried to block out the reality of these children, to replace them with others who might be in her future, hidden just around the bend of events that had not yet happened. The children she could eradicate. The man, however, remained.

Shaking her head, Elaina told herself to stop being a fool. With effort, she concentrated on drawing Petey alone, a gift for Terri's birthday. She drew his round little-boy face, the baggy sweater hanging down over his knees, the rolled sleeves that kept threatening to fall over his hands, and the drooping socks, one of which was dangling half off him, draping onto the flagstones of the patio.

Flipping the page over, she started in on Betsy, working quickly because she knew the baby rarely stood still for long. Any second now, her legs would collapse and she'd be off on her hands and knees, galloping after a butterfly or simply playing with the bells on her new shoes. As it was, her expressions were as ephemeral as mist in the wind and as difficult to capture. Her plump body was a joy to draw, though, all curves and begging for sweeps of the pencil, voluptuous turns of the wrist—simplified technique that made the work go fast. Her bibbed overalls with straps crossed in back demanded the only straight lines and angles, and Elaina swiftly sketched them in before turning the page.

And then she drew Brad. Like a child savoring dessert, she had saved the best for last. The moment she began to sketch in the elegant outline of his head, though, she knew she could draw him over and over and never satisfy herself completely, never capture whatever it was she wanted to have of him. It was too elusive, too illusory, and her skill was much to puny.

The strength of his profile demanded all she could give. The square chin, the column of his throat with the slight protrusion of his Adam's apple, the slope of his shoulder and upper arm as he held his hands out toward Petey, tilting them to provide the little boy with a better angle for picking up the strings, all came under her careful scrutiny. But it was his lips that gave her the most trouble. There was no way she could depict the power she knew was there, and the tenderness, and the sweetness. Page after page flipped over as she tried to get it just right. His eyes. She couldn't see them, only his profile, but she knew them by heart. She sketched until her fingers cramped and then sketched some more, trying to collect as many of his expressions as she could against the day that she would see him no more. She was still working when the oven timer went off, a monotonous ping, ping, ping that was as much of an intrusion on intimacy as Brad's beeper had ever been.

Scrambled eggs, crisp bacon, and corn bread with warm syrup got rave reviews, and Petey enjoyed a second breakfast along with the adults.

Brad ate hungrily, too, but Elaina found her appetite strangely absent. Her stomach fluttered each time she looked up and found him looking at her. Always, his gaze lingered on her face, and always he responded to her voice, giving her his total attention when she spoke, as if her words were important to him. Still, though, she detected the same confusion in him that had been present when he left her in the bathroom. Mixed with that confusion was a warmth and a yearning that so closely complemented her own emotions, she found herself wishing Terri and Petey would go, that Betsy would fall asleep, and that she and Brad could gravitate to each other's arms again.

While the adults sipped their third cups of coffee and watched the children playing on the warm flagstones of the patio, Brad took Elaina's hand under the table, holding it on his lap while he talked charmingly to Terri. Elaina barely heard his words, was scarcely aware of Petey lifting off Betsy's sun hat and saying "Boo!" while Betsy squealed with delight.

When Petey grew tired of the game, Besty lifted her hat up herself and shouted, "Boo!" to her admiring audience. Elaina dragged herself out of her dream state to reach down and lift the baby up, hugging her tightly.

"That makes three words," she said, immensely proud. "Brad, don't forget to tell Margo when you go back today."

He laced his hands behind his head and stuck his long legs out in front of him, ankles crossed. "I'm not going back today. Nor tomorrow, either. I am free for two full, glorious days." Slowly, his gaze raked over her, a smile lurking in the depths of his eyes. She realized that he wanted to spend those two glorious days with her, and knew just as well that those days would each be twenty-four hours long. As she met his gaze over Betsy's head, her heart was hammering hard in her chest. If they were to spend the time together, she knew the days—and the nights—would be just as glorious for her.

Terri got to her feet and began noisily gathering dishes together.

"So what do you plan to do with your time off?" she asked, stacking plates one on top of another.

"I was thinking of taking these two lovely ladies out for a long drive today," he said, lifting Betsy and bouncing her on his knee. "Maybe up to Crater Lake." His gaze slid sideways to Elaina's face. "Ever been there?" She shook her head, and he smiled at her before turning again to Terri. "Would you like to join us?"

She laughed. "Not on your life! Mountain roads don't appeal to me. Thanks anyway. And I have a better idea. Why don't you leave Betsy with me? That way the two of you won't have to worry about her and you'll have a much nicer time."

"Oh, no, we couldn't!" Elaina said, but she was swiftly overruled.

"Thanks," Brad said, standing up. "You've just earned yourself a free appendectomy, lady."

Terri laughed again. "Now, aren't you lucky. I had one when I was twelve, so I can't hold you to it." She gathered up the sweater and socks that Petey had peeled off as the sun grew warm, and said briskly, "Let's collect what Betsy will need, love. We get to take her home with us for the day." She smiled slyly and added, "And the night, if it comes to that."

Brad laughed. "No, no. We'll be home by midnight, if that's not too late for you. I'm a working stiff and I've been up for a long time already. By midnight I'll be ready for bed. I would like a chance to take Lainie out for a leisurely dinner though, if you're game to baby-sit that late."

"No problem," Terri assured him.

"But it's your birthday!" protested Elaina.

"Oh, pooh, what does that mean?" One by one Elaina's arguments were shot down until Betsy and Terri and Petey had disappeared through the gate in the hedge and Brad was grinning at the success of his plan. Meeting his eyes, Elaina had to grin, too, a smile that just grew bigger and bigger and bigger until she thought she might burst with the happiness of the day.

"It's so blue!" Elaina stood on the edge of an overlook and surveyed the intensely sapphire blue lake that had been formed millenia before when Mount Masama blew its top.

"How can it be such a color?" she asked, turning to Brad. "It's as if it has gathered up the sky and magnified it a thousand times."

"I'm told that its depth, nearly two thousand feet, has a lot to do with the color. And the shape of the crater helps too." Brad turned her back around again and wrapped his arms around her from behind, protecting her from the chill of the high, thin air. "And look, see the minicrater in

Wizard Island? That fascinates me. A volcano within a volcano."

"How long since it's blown?" Elaina asked, feeling for the first time a hint of apprehension. She remembered when Mount St. Helens had blown its top, and the devastation that had followed.

"You just read it in the book," he reminded her comfortingly. "Six thousand, six hundred years ago." He rubbed his hands up and down her arms, erasing the goose bumps. "It's considered safely extinct. Of course," he added slyly, "there is that hot spring at Klamath Falls. That shows there's some part of the earth's core not far from here that's still cooking away."

"Thanks a lot," she said, shoving her hands into the pockets of her dress. He wrapped his fingers around her wrists and pulled her hands free.

"Hey," he said softly, "leave room for joy, remember?" Tilting her head back, she smiled at him.

"I remember."

He gazed into her eyes for a moment, then kissed her hard on the mouth, filling her with joy but taking her by surprise. The intensity of her own swift and heated response also took her by surprise. At the first touch of his tongue she flowered for him, a small sound in the back of her throat telling him of her pleasure. His hands cupped and massaged her breasts, and she felt her nipples stiffen, as he found them through the fabrics that covered them, tugging at them with thumbs and forefingers. One hand moved down her body and she arched toward it, accepting his caress as he drew her tightly back against him, curving his fingers over the roundness below her belly. She gasped and surged against him, all her senses awake to his touch, her entire body yearning for more and more.

"Lainie . . . Lainie . . ." He turned her to face him. The green of his eyes had softened to a deep glow, and his mouth was curved into a tender smile that warmed her insides. Cradling her head in his hands, he kissed her again, angling his mouth across hers. His tongue plundered deep as he moved his body in a slow, sensuous rhythm against her. She slid her arms around his waist, feeling the hard muscles of his back, the heat of his body, the trembling in his limbs as he held her firmly against the cradle of his hips.

There was no time, no earth, no reality but that of touching each other, tasting each other. The reality was soft whispers, sighs, and gentle moans as the sensations became unbearably poignant and they were forced to take a time out. They clung to each other and smiled, and took tiny, replenishing sips from each other's lips.

The sound of voices coming down the trail brought them back to the world. Brad turned her from him again, holding her as before, her back pressed to his front, his chin near her ear, her head on his shoulder. She wrapped her arms over his, holding them close under her breasts, her hands curled around his hard elbows.

"Speaking of volcanic eruptions," he murmured as the voices came nearer. "You have the most potent kisses in the world, Elaina McIvor!"

"*I* do?" she whispered. "What about you?"

"It's not me," he said. "It's all your doing. When you kiss me I forget where I am, what I'm supposed to be doing. Hell, who I am, even!"

The sound of several pairs of hiking boots crunching on the gravel made her move restlessly in his arms. She, too, had forgotten where they were and what they were supposed to be doing for however long they had had the overlook to themselves. But now they no longer had it to themselves and should act like responsible adults, not randy teenagers. She knew her face was turning redder and redder, and she said in a low, urgent voice, "Brad, let me go."

"You stay still," he hissed in her ear. "You got me into this state, so you're not going to go away and leave me . . . um, exposed to the mocking eyes of the world." He moved against her again, making her tinglingly aware that his "state" was still very much in evidence. An uncharacteristic giggle rose inside her as she was struck by the humor of the situation—his situation. She slithered out of his arms and darted away, leaving him hugging nothing but the guardrail that kept the unwary from slipping off the crumbly, volcanic rock trail and sliding down the sheer side of the crater to the water two thousand feet below.

"Oh, look, Brad," she said from several yards away. "That must be the Phantom Ship we read about in the booklet you bought. Come over here. There's a much better view without that tree in the way."

"I'm fine right here," he said, but even as he lowered his brows in a scowl, she could see the laughing light in his eyes.

Long past the time when he must surely have been able to move without embarrassment he stood leaning on the railing, watching her. She could feel his gaze on her, but refused to turn, keeping her attention instead on the beautiful scene below. She watched the changing light and shadows create mosaics on crater walls, on lake, and on islands, and breathed in the clean, sharp air, delighting in the silence as the view point was left to them again.

About to go back to where Brad stood, Elaina turned and was startled to see another man close by, tall and athletic, in hiking shorts and boots. He had a bushy mustache and a gleam of interest in his eye. "Well, hi, there," he said. "Nice view." His manner suggested that she was part of what made it nice.

Elaina agreed that it was, and made to step past him. The trail was narrow here, though, and short of giving him a shove, there was no way to do it. She wasn't certain that he was deliberately keeping her there, but she suspected he might be. His eyes glittered as he continued to gaze at her.

"You look like a lady who could use some company on the trail," he said, shifting the straps of his backpack to a more comfortable position. "And I'm just the guy to provide it. Walk with me?" He held out a hand.

"Thanks," she said, "but I already have the company I want." She cast a glance over at Brad where he still stood, half obscured by a pine tree, watching quietly, making no move to interfere. But she knew without having to think about it that if he felt she was unable to handle things, he'd be at her side in one second.

The man's gaze followed hers and his mouth twisted into a rueful grimace. "Oops, sorry," he said. "I thought you were alone. My mistake. No offence, buddy. Forgive me, miss."

"Nothing to forgive," she told him as he backed off and left her room to regain a solid footing on the main trail. "Enjoy your hike."

"Yeah, you too." As he walked away, he paused for one backward glance and a small wave.

Brad took her hand in his, swinging them between them as they walked back the way they'd come.

"It was nice of you not to interfere," she said. "Kirk would have . . . uh, it was nice of you. Thanks. I like to think I can take care of myself."

He squeezed her fingers. "I don't just think you can. I know it. Besides, I knew there was no chance you'd go off hiking with him."

"Confident, aren't you?"

He was silent for a moment, then said, "Yeah. With you, I do feel confident that you won't do anything to make me feel small. It's a nice feeling." Startled by his serious treatment of her light words, she made no reply, and he went on.

"It wasn't like that during my marriage. LeeAnn liked to keep me on edge. If a guy had made her an offer like that, she might have taken him up on it. If he noticed me, she could just as easily as not pretend that she didn't know me, or that I was her brother, or even that I'd been following her and she was glad of his protection. She was the confident one. She knew I'd never let her out of my sight in a situation like that. So she was safe doing what she did. Later, she would have said it was all a joke and that I was too stuffy and staid and had no sense of humor. She was happiest when she had more than one man following her, vying for her attention."

They were back at the car as he finished and he let her hand go while he unlocked the door and saw her seated. They were using her car today, as if was more reliable and comfortable than his rattletrap van. To her surprise, when they had left her house he had walked to the passenger side, not making any suggestion that he should drive. When she'd asked if he would, since he knew where they were going and she didn't, he'd walked around to the other side and taken the keys from her. His smile told her that she had pleased him with the offer.

Now, he got behind the wheel as if that were where he belonged.

"We can drive all the way around the lake," he said. "The Rim Drive is worth seeing. Okay with you?"

Anything he wanted to do was okay with her, and she smiled her agreement and snuggled up under his arm.

As they slowly drove clockwise along the paved road that kept traffic moving one way around the rim, they came to many different vantage points. At each one Brad stopped so they could fill their senses with the beauty of the lake, and with the temptation of each other's lips. The sun had gone down and as dusk approached, the shadows deepened, turning the scene into one of magic and mystery. The color of the lake turned to indigo, and Wizard Island and the Phantom Ship were inky black outlines in the darkening depths of the crater.

At Rim Village, they stopped for dinner in the rustic inn, Crater Lake Lodge, enjoying roast beef and crusty potatoes served with a rich, thick gravy and tender-crisp carrots. The charming waitress grinned when Elaina commented on how nicely the vegetables were cooked, and confessed that that was about the greatest degree of doneness the chef could get on carrots at that altitude, where water boiled at considerably less than two hundred twelve degrees.

They lingered long over their wine, Brad filling her glass twice for every time he filled his. "I'm driving," he said firmly when she pointed out that she was getting more than her share. She liked that about him. He was not a man to take unnecessary risks with his own life or hers, or the lives of the unsuspecting motorists who might be coming around the next corner. She supposed he had seen the dire results of drinking and driving too often during his tenure in the emergency room to drink and drive himself. Still, it was nice to feel so safe with a man. Come to think of it, there was nothing, so far, that she didn't like about him.

The dining room was nearly empty when they were served their coffee. Brad sipped his, smiling at her over his cup.

Then, with a suddenness that shocked her, he asked, "Was Kirk your husband, Elaina?"

"What—what gives you the idea I was ever married?" she asked in a strangled voice, playing for time. She'd thought he'd missed her inadvertent reference to Kirk when he'd failed to say anything earlier.

"I don't know," he said, taking her hand and rubbing his thumb over her fingers as if feeling for the depression left by a wedding band. It had once existed, but she was glad now that it was gone. His gaze held hers over the flickering light of the candle. "But you were, weren't you?"

"Brad . . . It's not a time of my life I like to talk about. It was over three years ago and I prefer to leave it that way."

"I know you do," he said softly, still rubbing his thumb over her knuckles. "But I want to know you, Lainie. I want to know all about you. So tell me. Please?"

"I was married," she said in a strained voice, "and yet I wasn't. I met Kirk shortly after I moved to Indianapolis. I was twenty-three, fresh out of college and working in the Civic Library. He used to come in to check back issues in our periodical files. He sold advertising space for a company that published a large number of magazines. We talked, he discovered that I was a newcomer and offered to show me around. I was a very young, very naive twenty-three and was flattered that an older man was interested in me."

"How long were you with him, Lainie?"

"Five years." Her voice was little more than a whisper, and Brad knew it hurt her to reveal this part of her life. He wanted to tell her it didn't matter, that he didn't need to know, but something within him insisted that he did need to.

"Do you still love him?"

She shook her head. "No." Now, she smiled. "No, not even a little bit. But I did then and I feel very, very foolish about what happened. As I said, Kirk sold advertising space. Mostly for trade journals, and that meant he had to do a lot of traveling. He was away for half of each week. Sometimes more."

"That can be hard on a relationship," Brad said.

She nodded in agreement. "It was, but I had my job in the library and I was doing quite a bit of illustrating even then, so I kept busy. I wanted a family, but he didn't. Of course, I understand now why he didn't, but then he had me convinced it was because I'd be a poor mother." She pulled a wry face and slipped her hand free. She tucked it onto her lap with her other one and looked down, not meeting his eyes.

"We were saving for our dream house, and then one day when he was in Cincinnati, I learned that we wouldn't have to save any more. By mail I had played the lottery run in another state. I'd been doing that for some time. A silly habit really. But that day it paid off. I won a hundred thousand dollars in the lottery and was too excited to wait until he got home the next day to tell him. I called his hotel, even though he had always made it a very firm rule that I was never to call him there unless it was a life-and-death emergency." She looked at him again. "Can you believe that for five years I was a good, obedient little . . . woman and had never once called him there? Five years!

"Anyway, it was a good thing I hadn't ever needed him during those years, because it turned out that they had never heard of him at that hotel or any of the other hotels I called that day. Do you have any idea how many hotels and motels there are in Cincinnati?"

Brad knew the question didn't require a response, so he just smiled at her encouragingly, wishing again that he had never asked her to tell him this story. The strain of it was clear on her face, in the taut line of her mouth, the set of her shoulders.

"I called every one of them," she said, shaking her head at the memory. "And then I called his office to see if maybe he had gone to a different city. But no, his boss's secretary confirmed that he was in Cincinnati. When I explained that he wasn't staying in the hotel he normally used, but with friends and I'd lost the number he'd given me, she checked the records and gave me a number to try.

"A little child answered and when I asked for Kirk, she called out, 'Mommy, it's for Daddy. Will he be home tonight?' "

For the first time, Brad detected a quaver in her voice. He wanted desperately to hold her, to comfort her and ease her pain, but he sat very still, afraid to break the flow of her words.

"A woman came on and said she was Kirk's wife and could she take a message. I don't know why I didn't hang up right then, but stupidly I said that she couldn't be his wife because I was. She thought I was some kind of sicko and laughed at me. She said that since she was the mother of his three children aged five through ten, she figured her wifehood took precedence over mine, and suggested I find some other marriage to try to break up, because hers was as solid as the Rock of Gibraltar, thank you very much, and hung up."

Elaina looked at Brad with eyes that seemed bruised and bewildered as if she was feeling again the shock and disbelief and terrible betrayal she had suffered then.

She drew in a shuddering breath. "That was the kind of trust she had in him. And the kind of trust I had in him too. I was sure there was some kind of weird mistake, and that it would all get sorted out. I didn't believe it until he came home the next day and berated me for having phoned him at that number. He demanded to know how I had gotten it, accused me of having known all along and of wanting to 'ruin' things for him. He couldn't seem to grasp that he had more than just ruined things for me. To this day, I'm sure he doesn't know what he did to me."

"Ah, Lainie. That was so lousy for you. He hurt you a lot."

She nodded.

"So what did you do? I hope you took your hundred grand and sued the pants off him!"

Elaina laughed, surprised to discover that she could, that what had happened three years ago no longer seemed like such a tragedy. "I didn't want his pants. I didn't want him anymore. I didn't even turn him in to the law. If his wife wanted to do that, then I felt it was up to her. I just took my hundred grand and headed west. Isn't that what a person's supposed to do when life in the east becomes unbearable?"

He stood and helped her up, then put some money on the tray with the check. He said nothing until they were outside in the parking lot. "And how bearable has your life become in the last three years?" he asked, sliding a hand up under her hair.

She looked at him. She was aware of the warmth of him close to her, the magnetism of his eyes, the almost palpable tension and electricity flowing between her body and his.

"Why don't you ask me how bearable it's become in the past few weeks?" she said, feeling frightened and excited and weak, but wanting him to know. If he didn't already.

He drew in his breath and met her gaze. His fingers tightened on the nape of her neck as he pulled her so near she could feel his breath on her face. He smiled crookedly and his hand trembled against her. "I don't think I dare to ask right now," he said. "How 'bout I do it when we're down off this mountain again? I think the altitude's getting to me."

But the look in his eyes told her that he was on as much of a high as she was, and that it had nothing to do with altitude at all.

Nine

They drove down the mountain in silence. On the long road home, their only contact was their linked hands and the excitement that ebbed and flowed and swirled around them. Desire rippled through Elaina, heating her inner self. She sighed quietly now and then, wanting to curl up in his arms and burrow her face against the fragrance of his skin. That they were destined to make love that night was in no doubt in her mind. That he wanted her as much as she wanted him was something she took as a given. She loved him. The knowledge filled her with euphoria. Even if his feelings were different, not as strong as hers, it couldn't lessen what she felt for him, couldn't detract from her deep need to share herself fully with him.

They picked up Betsy at Terri's and hurried to her house. There was a certain constraint about Brad as he unlocked the door and carried in all of Betsy's bits and pieces. Elaina gently laid the sleeping baby in the crib and tucked her blankets close around her. She turned to find Brad's gaze on her, and smiled tenderly at him. The smile faded, though, as she realized that somewhere on the trip home, he had lost the joy they had found together. Maybe, she thought, it had only been the altitude after all. For him.

Yet as soon as they were in the living room, he wrapped his hands around her arms and drew her close. "Elaina," he said, then fell silent, his face grave, his eyes somber. She could feel the tension in his hands as they trembled on her upper arms.

She didn't know what was wrong, only that something was. Nor did she know how to fix it, only that she had to try. "What is it?" she asked, moving in closer. She put her arms around him, holding him gently as she tried to ease whatever distress he was feeling.

He resisted her at first, tried to push her away, but it was a weak push. His body was already rising in response to her closeness. Helplessly, he pulled her tight against him, closing his eyes as if in pain. "We have to talk," he murmured. "Lainie, move away from me."

His obvious desire triggered her own, which had never been far below the surface since she had met him. She was as unable as he to withstand its power. "Later," she said, moving her mouth over his.

With a groan of surrender, he took her lips in a deep and stirring kiss. His hands were strong on her back, slowly moving downward until he cupped her buttocks, drawing her high and hard against him. His lips were firm as he moved them over hers, and his tongue caressed the roof of her mouth with little darting motions, eliciting soft moans from deep within her.

Clutching at his shirt, she felt the heavy pounding of his heart. She slid the buttons out of their holes, one by one, touching the soft pelt of hair. He was so hot! His skin was burning. She cooled it with her tongue and he shuddered. He tilted his head back to give her access to his throat, then swooped over her again to kiss her mouth and run his hands into her hair, holding her head still while he plundered deeply, making her arch up against him.

He held the kiss while he unzipped her dress and slid it down over her shoulders, revealing her rounded softness in the sheer, lacy teddy she wore. He met her shy gaze, his own eyes dark with the desire he saw clearly reflected in her face. He touched her taut nipples with the tips of his fingers, then bent and drew one, along with its covering of silk, into his mouth. He kissed the other one, too, and then looked at her flushed face and limpid eyes. Her chest was heaving, her lips parted and tremulous, as he slowly slid down the straps of the teddy and bared her to the waist.

She took his hands and placed them over her breasts, holding them to her. "I love you,, Brad," she said softly.

He made a harsh, broken sound and pulled her against him again, rocking her in his arms, his cheek on her soft hair. "Oh, Lainie, Lainie," he whispered finally. "I want so badly to stay."

"I want you to say," she said, moving her hands

up to his shoulders. She tilted back to look into his eyes, and the tips of her breasts rubbed sensuously against his chest. But he moved back, holding her away from him, and she didn't know what to do.

If there was anything more to be said at a time like this, she didn't know what it might be. She only continued to gaze into his eyes, seeing the longing there, the storm of indecision, the confusion he was battling.

"But I can't," he said, his voice strained.

Elaina stared at him. What was happening? Why was he doing this? He wanted her. She knew that. And he knew she wanted him. She had just told him she loved him, baring her soul to him as well as her body.

She let her hands fall from him. "Why?" she managed to ask.

Still holding her by the shoulders, his eyes locked with hers, he said, "Because I'm falling in love with you, Elaina. And because it has to stop right here before it goes any further. Oh, hell, what am I saying? I'm not just falling in love with you, I have fallen. But you've had one bad experience with a rat. I don't want to be responsible for giving you another one."

She stepped back from him, rubbing her hands up and down her arms, trying to erase the memory of his touch. "Are you a rat?" Numbly, she pulled her clothing back up.

"If I took what you're offering, I would be." He drew in a deep breath, then blurted out. "I don't want to get married, Elaina!"

She recoiled with shock. "I don't recall asking

you to marry me," she said through the agony slicing her heart. She saw the brick-colored flush rise on his face again.

"No. Of course you didn't. But isn't it what you'd expect of a man who loved you? Isn't it what you expected before?"

"Yes, it's what I expected before, but I was twenty-three then, and naive. I thought love and marriage were inseparable. But what kind of a marriage did that belief get me? You know the answer to that. Kirk married me because he liked having a wife to take care of him. He was spending as much time in Indianapolis as he was in Cincinnati, and he didn't like living in hotels. He went through that phony ceremony so that he'd have a place to stay, someone to cook and clean and fill his bed at night. A girlfriend has to be treated better than a wife. A lover expects to be taken out and wined and dined and danced until dawn. But not a wife. I was a convenience to him. Someone to look after him. I'm delighted to know that you don't want that same convenience, Brad. It warms my heart!"

"Lainie—" He paused, swallowed hard, then said softly, "Don't. Please don't." He lifted one hand as if to touch her, then dropped it to his side.

"Don't what?"

"Put yourself down. You think I'm putting you down, don't you? You think that after all we shared today, after the unspoken promises we made to each other, that I'm rejecting you. I'm not, love. It isn't like that."

She had nothing to say. He was right. That was what she thought. She had believed he wanted her, had made it as plain as she knew how that she wanted him, and still he was leaving. If that wasn't rejection, she didn't know what was. She shrugged and stepped past him.

"Then you'd better go," she said, opening the door for him. "You said this morning that your day started early. You must be tired."

"Oh, Lainie. Dammit, how can I make you understand?" He shoved the door shut, his chest rising and falling rapidly as he stared down at her. His mouth was taut and deep lines ran from his nose to the corners of his lips.

"You don't have to make me understand anything," she said. "I understand perfectly well. I'm not stupid. You're afraid of commitment and you think that's what I'd demand of you. You're wrong, but I know you won't believe that, so there's nothing more to say."

"Lainie, that's the trouble. I do believe it. But don't you see? You'd have every right to expect me to marry you, and when I didn't, it wouldn't be what you deserve. It wouldn't be fair. I—I love you too much to want to do that to you. I . . . oh, damn, Lainie, I'm sorry."

He opened the door and stepped out, then closed it firmly behind him.

For a long time Elaina stood there, staring blankly at the white wood panels, at the dull gleam of the brass doorknob, at the Yale lock that had clicked into place. Then, numb and half blind, she walked to the bathroom, turned on the shower and, leaving her clothes in a heap on the floor, stepped into the pounding, hot spray. She didn't wash herself, but simply let the water run over her as if it could dilute her pain. But nothing could dilute it, not the tears she eventually shed, not the great, wrenching sobs that tore from her, nor the pounding of her fists against the tiled wall.

When the water ran cold she turned it off and wrapped herself in a big towel. She rubbed her hair with another, blew her nose hard, and stopped her tears. She padded barefoot into her studio and found under the chair cushion the sketches she had made that morning. Switching on one of the angle lamps over her table, she perched on her high stool and spread them out. After flinging the small towel off her head, she simply sat and gazed at the drawings.

The one of Petey she set aside for Terri, having forgotten to give it to her as a birthday gift. The one of Betsy she mounted carefully on a mat and slipped it into a cardboard frame, ready to send it to Margo in the morning. The others she simply looked at helplessly, wanting to crumple them one by one and consign them to the trash basket, but knowing she never could. They were too important to her. Brad was too important to her. But how could she make him see that?

She studied each drawing as if within it there might be the secret she needed. But even after half an hour of scrutinizing the expressions of his she had captured, each plane and angle of his face, she was no closer to knowing than she had been when she started. All she knew was that she loved him and wanted him, and that there was no way to make her dreams come true without him.

Finally, she gathered up the dozen or so different images she had made of him and laid them carefully in a drawer, setting a fresh pad of drawing paper over them to hide them from her own sight.

Harrison was prowling the room restlessly, then sat beside the door to the patio, hidden behind the drawn drapes. He gave her his let-me-out-right-this-minute meow, and yowled plaintively when she was slow to respond.

"All right, all right," she said, unlocking the door and pushing it aside for him. "Go on out then, but don't take all night about it."

It was a warm night, she realized as she followed the cat onto the patio, letting the drapes fall shut behind her.

"Lainie?" Brad's soft voice came from the darkness near the umbrella table.

"What are you doing back here?" She was surprised that she sounded so calm. Inside she was shaking and in pain from the ice grinding through her blood.

He stood, a dim shape looming as he took one step toward her. "I never left. I sat in the van for a while, then came to the door. But I couldn't ring the bell. So I walked around here. I heard your shower running."

She wondered if he had also heard her weeping.

"I never wanted to hurt you like that, Lainie," he said, moving closer, and she knew he had. She backed up, then stopped. Why should she pretend that he hadn't hurt her? Did she lack even the courage for that?

"Could I come in now?" he asked.

"Are you sure you want to?"

"Ah, Lainie. I'm sure I want to. What I have to know is—is that still what you want?"

Through the pain in her throat, she said, "I think I made myself clear an hour or more ago. But I refuse to beg. I'm going in. You suit yourself."

With that, she strode back through the door, sweeping the drapes aside and not looking to see if he followed her. But when she crashed into the side of her drawing table, flying blind, he was there to catch and steady her.

Stiff, she refused to turn and face him.

"Oh, hell, Lainie, you aren't going to make this easy for me, are you? No, of course you aren't. So there's only one way."

He snatched her towel from her and dragged her back against him, running his warm hands down over her naked flesh, kissing her neck, her ear, her cheek, his mouth finding the wet streaks of her tears. Then she was turned and he was rocking her close in his arms.

"I love you," he said. He wiped her face dry with his thumbs, placing tiny kisses on her eyelids and cheeks and nose. "I don't know if that's going to be enough for you, Lainie, but if you're willing to give us a try on that basis, then I want you and I need you and I'll do everything in my power not to hurt you again."

She couldn't speak, could only nod. He lifted her into his arms and carried her toward her bedroom.

"Put me down. I'm too big for you to carry."

He laughed, a soft, sexy, warm sound that filled her with joy. "You're not big, my love. You're tall. But I'm a whole lot taller." He laid her in the center of the bed and turned on the lamp on the bedside table. He stood erect, his gaze sweeping over her slim yet rounded form.

Her whole body was suffused by a pink flush and her eyes were shy as she tried to be brave under his scrutiny. She thrilled him and delighted him and pleased him in every way.

"You are the most beautiful woman I have ever seen," he said with such simple sincerity that she had to believe him.

"Brad . . ." Her breathing was stifled as she forced herself to lie still under his avid gaze. She had never felt beautiful before in her life, yet now she did. She loved it, but it still embarrassed her to have him looking at her that way while he stood over her fully clothed. Kirk had never stared at her, and she hadn't wanted him to.

Nor had she stared at him as she did at Brad as he carelessly ripped off his clothing. She watched, running her tongue over her lips as he slid his zipper down, the sound of it rippling through her on a new wave of desire. He lifted one foot and tugged at the laces of his shoe, pulled it and the sock off, then did the other one. Then, hooking his thumbs into his waistband, he pulled his pants off, leaving himself clad only in a pair of pale blue bikini shorts that did little to hide the burgeoning shape within. Slowly, his gaze on her face as if he were afraid she might suddenly show distaste or fear, or bolt from the room, he approached the bed. He knelt on it beside her and waited for her to make the next move.

She knew her eyes were wide. Her lips were parted and dry with the breath that rasped in and out over them. She moistened them with the tip of her tongue and trembled, filled with a burning need for him, aching with a yearning that knew no depth, bursting with love for this man.

Rising up on one elbow, she lifted her hand and touched that pulsing flesh under the pale blue cloth. It jumped under her fingers and he closed his eyes, drawing in a sharp breath. He opened them again when she moved. As she knelt before him he caught her face in his hands. He kissed her over and over until he parted her lips with his own. His tongue plunged deep inside, dipping and withdrawing in an ancient rhythm that was only a prelude for what was to come.

She raked her nails lightly down his back, was rewarded by his shudder of pleasure, and hooked her fingers under the elastic of his shorts. Slowly, carefully she eased them down over his slim hips and rocklike thighs, then, as he lowered himself to the bed, over his legs and off his feet. Swallowing the huge lump in her throat, she moved back from him and took her time examining him.

"Lainie," he gasped, when she eluded his reaching hand. "Lainie, please!"

His eyes were half shut, green glints shining from between thick, short lashes. His cheeks were flushed and the cords in his throat stood out, pulse hammering wildly beside one of them. The curling hairs on his chest tapered to an arrow that flared out once more as it went lower, darkened, grew thicker. His proud manhood stood out from that nest, moving as she gazed at it, as if beckoning her. His legs were strong and tanned and well sprinkled with the same dark curls that covered his chest. His feet were long and narrow, the toes straight with square, short nails.

Running her gaze back up, she lingered again at that most fascinating portion of his anatomy, that place where he most differed from her. His breathing grew more agitated, and his fists were clenched by his sides. His eyes, fully open now, were pleading with her to stop this teasing and come to him. But he didn't move, leaving it all up to her now.

"You are beautiful too," she whispered, touching him at last. She laid her hand over his pounding heart, feeling one small, pebble-hard nipple press into her palm. "I want to draw you like this."

As if she might leave, he clapped his hand over hers and pinned it to her chest. "Not now!"

With a breathless laugh, she agreed. "No. Not now. But someday?"

"God, yes, anything." He slid his hand up over her hip, drawing her closer. She fell from her knees, her body draping across his, and was captured as he covered her mouth with his.

Her breasts, flattened against his chest, ached, and she cried out with the sweet pain of it. His hands stroked up her sides and curved around her breasts, and she arched to press them into his palms. "I love that," she gasped. He squeezed and massaged and tugged on her nipples.

"And that?" he murmured. "Tell me everything you like, love. I want to give you so much pleasure."

"I love everything you do to me," she said.

He rolled her onto her back, burying his face between her breasts, his thumbs and fingers still plucking and stroking. Then his mouth was covering one hard rosy tip and she sobbed with the pleasure of it. Fiery sensations zinged through her to her core, where they pulsed and swelled and heated her almost to the boiling point. One of his large, hard hands caressed her body, cupping, caressing, smoothing over silken skin, parting her thighs to stroke the softness there before moving on. His mouth followed the track his hand had made, and like his fingers paused to caress the sensitive skin behind her knee and the arch of her foot, then began the long, slow journey upward again.

"Brad, please," she whispered. "I want you."

"Soon, darling, soon." He knew his own swiftly rising excitement, made greater by her eager response to his caresses, must make it very soon. But he wanted to worship her longer, to pleasure her more. He pressed her legs apart and knelt between them. His hands slipped up her thighs, over her abdomen to her breasts, massaging their softness and squeezing her hard nipples, reveling in the different textures she offered him.

As his mouth skimmed down over her belly, she writhed and tossed under his hands, sobbing with desire. The moment his tongue parted the dampness between her thighs, though, she stiffened, going rigid with shock and lifting herself up on her elbows.

"Brad?" Her voice was high and wild, her eyes filled with disbelief as he raised his head. He soothed her with gentle hands, smiling at her, murmuring to her, his voice soft and persuasive. Could it be that no man had ever . . . ? No! Yet her expression told him it was so.

"It's okay, Lainie," he crooned, resting his cheek against her abdomen, stroking her with his fingers.

"But . . ."

"I love you. I'm going to kiss you, sweetheart. I won't hurt you. And I promise it will be good for you. You'll like it, Lainie. Please." Gently, he slipped his arms around her again and lowered her back to the mattress. Stroking, caressing, he patiently rebuilt the waves of delight within her until she was soft and pliant in his arms, gasping for breath again, arching up to his touch. This time, when he gave her that most intimate of kisses, she did not flinch away, but cried out, her fist stuffed against her mouth, her head rolling from side to side on the pillow. And then she was flying far, far away from everything familiar, but the place she flew to was so wondrous and beautiful she never wanted to leave it again.

She only realized she was crying when she became aware of Brad speaking her name over and over again, and begging her not to cry.

She wiped her eyes on the corner of the pillow case, then looked at him and drew in a tremulous breath.

"Are you all right?" he asked, his face pale as he hovered over her protectively.

Her voice was still thick with sobs and tears as she said, "I don't know. What—what happened to me, Brad?" She was shaking as if in shock.

He gave her a strange look, then tugged the comforter up from the foot of the bed and tucked it around them. "What do you mean, what happened to you?"

"Well . . . it was strange. You were . . ." She

paused, her eyes widening as she remembered what he had been doing. She knew she was blushing, and forced herself to go on. "You were . . . kissing me . . . like that and then I seemed to get lost. I don't know where it was, but it was all full of beautiful colors and maybe music and I couldn't breathe, but then I didn't have to and it was the most incredible thing that's ever happened to me. I don't know why I cried."

"Dammit, Lainie," he said, gulping hard. "You make me want to cry! You honestly don't know, do you? Sweetheart, you had a climax. And if it was the first one you've ever had you were well and truly cheated by that lying, cheating bigamist and I—Oh, hell, Elaina, what am I going to do with you?"

She touched his face, rubbing her fingers over the slight beard on his chin, smoothing out the lines at the corners of his eyes, and smiled. "I don't know," she whispered. "But since you did it once, why don't you see if you can do it again?"

Ten

He laughed and pulled the comforter off her body, his hands creating little currents and swirls of sensation. His gaze lingered on her glowing skin like a caress, then he touched each place he gazed upon with warm and gentle lips.

Slowly, as before, he brought her to the edge of ecstasy until she cried out his name and arched against him. When she lost her natural inhibitions and began to return his caresses, he encouraged her with soft words and praise. Yet when her hair swept across the tops of his thighs and her kisses grew bolder and bolder, he stiffened. Tangling his hands in her hair, he drew her head back up to his chest.

"Another time, love," he whispered hoarsely, "and I won't say no, but not this time. Lie back, Lainie. I need to get ready for you now."

She was just beginning to feel chilled when he wrapped her in his warmth again, his arms and his legs and his mouth generating a heat that filled her as his body filled her. And then they were soaring together to a higher delight than had ever existed, until the world went black and they fell together into a silver cloud.

This time, her tears didn't worry him, and when she began to laugh several minutes later, he lifted himself up on his elbows and traced her mouth with one finger.

"I'd rather have you laughing after loving me than crying," he said. "But I'd kind of like to share the joke." He smiled at her as she opened her eyes.

Rolling off her, he nestled her close to his side. "Well? Share?"

"I was just thinking that I'm not entitled to all this joy."

His smile faded. "Why not?"

"No pockets."

He grinned and ran a hand down over her body. "You think not, huh? What about this pocket of joy?"

Her chuckle was sleepy and sated and music to him.

Long after she slept, he looked at her face, loving her, aching with the knowledge of what had to come.

He should leave now, he told himself. He should get out of this bed, put on his clothes, and never come back, because there was no solution to the problems they'd have if he stayed.

But I can't leave yet! I want her too much.

Oh, hell, Bradshaw, he argued with himself. *What are you doing? You know she needs a husband, kids. Put an end to it. It has to end, so make it now. Don't prolong the agony.* He stroked her hair back from her cheek and lashes, and saw her smile at his touch.

Then when, if not now? Give it a timetable. It wasn't going to get any easier. This wasn't an itch that once scratched would go away. This was real and powerful and not something to meddle with. She wasn't something to meddle with. So when?

When Margo was better? When Betsy went back to her? Yes. Then he'd break it off. He had to help her with the baby, didn't he? Of course he did!

Right. When Betsy goes home. Then you break it off. Deal? Deal! He switched off the lamp and lay back down, holding Elaina close. His heart was full of love and the ache he knew he would live with the rest of his lonely life.

"Hi, there," Brad said, when a small, warm body bounced on his back and a pair of tiny hands clasped his ears. He'd heard Elaina get up when Betsy had first stirred and called out. He had wanted her to stay with him, had resented the fact that she had to leave him and go to someone else's baby. Then he'd remembered that if it hadn't been for that baby, he wouldn't be in this warm, soft bed in the first place and last night never would have happened. Instead of resenting Betsy, he should be setting up an education fund for her or something as a reward.

He'd then recalled his promise to himself last

night. When Betsy went home, he would stop coming here. He'd groaned at the thought, and that was when Elaina dumped Betsy on his back.

Reaching back with one hand, he captured the baby around her middle and tumbled her onto the mattress beside him. He rolled over and sat her astride his chest. Looking up at Elaina, he said, "I suppose I should count myself lucky. My mom used to get Dad out of bed in the morning by dumping a wet baby in with him. You, at least, came up with a dry one."

"That's the only kind I had," she said lightly. "But I'll remember what your mother did for anoth—" She bit the word off and turned to go. He caught her hand and swung her back, pulling her down onto the bed.

"Elaina."

She met his eyes reluctantly.

"You were going to say, another time?"

She remained silent, and her gaze slid away from his again. He lifted her hand to his mouth and kissed her palm, her wrist, the inside of her elbow, dragging her closer until she was forced to meet his eyes. "Hey, lady. I told you last night that I love you. Nothing that happened has made me change my mind. I love you just as much today. No. More, probably. So unless you tell me there can't be, I'm hoping there will be many more times that I'll wake up in your bed."

He shifted Betsy to one side so he could sit higher and place a hard, hot kiss on Elaina's mouth. She sighed as she softened to him. "We have a joint responsibility," he said, "and as long as we have her, I'm afraid you're stuck with me."

After a moment of looking searchingly into his eyes, she nodded. "I can live with that." She said it, but she knew she lied. Because how could she go on living when she was no longer stuck with him?

Reprieve! The word rang through Elaina's mind a week and a half later as she drove to the hospital to pick up Margo. The infection had cleared, but she was still weak and depressed. She refused to allow the hospital to contact her parents, although they lived nearby. Brad had told Elaina that Margo hadn't spoken to her parents since before Betsy was born. And, he'd added, Margo couldn't possibly go back to her small apartment and her job of cleaning houses.

Although housework could be fun, Elaina reminded herself, thinking of yesterday when Brad had come in and found her vacuuming while Betsy slept. He had put his arms around her, helping her push the machine around. But when he had shut it off and walked her backward to the wicker couch, easing her down onto it, she had known housework was over.

"Don't you want to move to a bigger bed?" she asked.

"I don't want to move anywhere except deep inside you," he said, as he took off her T-shirt and unhooked her bra. Her nipples, responding as always to his words and his touch and his presence, were rigid, waiting for his kisses. He licked one, wetting it thoroughly, then blew on it, making the skin around it pucker, jutting it higher, turning it rosier. He took it deep into his mouth, sucking hard while she tugged his shirt out of the waist of his pants.

The couch wasn't made for two, which necessitated their staying very close together even as they slowly undressed each other. When she was completely naked in his arms, she wrapped herself around him, feeling the coarse hairs of his thighs tickle and tease the soft, sensitive skin of her own thighs. She scraped her nails down his back and over his buttocks, familiar now with the shape and texture of his body, but no less fascinated by it, no less appreciative.

"Come into me," she whispered urgently. "I need you so much!"

"Ah, love!" he sighed. He penetrated her deeply, swiftly, his gaze on her face. "Oh, Lainie, how I love you!"

"Brad, Brad!" she cried out as desire washed over her, making her dizzy and light-headed, filling her with frothy bubbles of delight. "I don't want this ever to end! I want . . . I wish . . ."

"Don't!" he gasped, and stopped her words with his mouth. Their heated bodies rushed them to completion, but they both knew that this time her tears were not tears of joy. Their time together was fast running out.

And minutes later he had asked her to take Margo into her home for a while.

When she picked up Margo at the hospital, she knew she was seeing Betsy as she would be in seventeen years—the same wispy blond hair, the same huge blue eyes, and the same round face as Betsy's characterized Margo's good looks. Elaina wanted to cuddle Margo as she cuddled Betsy.

When she got Margo home, the girl burst into tears at the sight of her baby daughter toddling unsteadily across the room toward her. And then Elaina *did* cuddle Margo.

"She's learned to walk," Margo said, still weeping. "When? I hate to have missed it."

"She took her first steps yesterday, and you *didn't* miss it."

Margo looked bewildered, but swiftly Elaina got a casette and pushed it into the VCR. Fascinated, Margo watched scenes of Betsy doing everything from playing with Petey to splashing Brad as he bathed her.

Later in the evening when Elaina tucked both Betsy and Betsy's mother into bed, she felt for the second time in her life like the mother of two. The very next morning, though, she realized she was the mother of none. She had to hide her tears, then, because it was to Margo that Betsy took her every need, her every little joy.

Margo stayed for a week, recovering, regaining strength, and if her presence in the house meant no privacy for Brad and Elaina, it meant, at least to Elaina, that Brad would continue to come daily. Although she knew that to lose Betsy and Margo would also mean losing Brad, she forced herself to do the right thing and encouraged the teenager to contact her family.

As the second week began, on Tuesday morning at breakfast, Margo finally agreed that the time was right. She would call her parents. When she did, things happened far too fast for Elaina. Within hours, a kind and loving couple arrived with hugs and kisses and forgiveness, and delight in their unknown grandchild. Then with a sickening abruptness, Elaina was alone.

The crib and the high chair belonged to Brad. Careful not to look around the room where there were no more baby clothes, no more toys, no more mobile hanging from the ceiling, Elaina took down the crib and carried it out to the front porch. She folded the high chair, added it to the stack outside, then closed the door firmly. She walked resolutely across the living room and into her studio, hearing the echoing emptiness of her house and the hollow roar in her mind. She was filled with the vast loneliness in her soul.

To block it, she unpacked the new work her publisher had assigned her and scanned the texts of the picture books, the first three of a series.

They were well written, aimed at three- to six-year-olds and, as did virtually all children's picture books, contained twenty-seven pages of text, three to four lines per page.

After reading the first one several times, Elaina was inspired to take out her pencils and begin some preliminary sketches. It was called *Julie's Baby Sister*, and it cried out for a plump, wispy-haired one-year-old who, no matter how Elaina tried to change it, always came out looking like Betsy. And Julie, contrary to what Elaina wanted, resembled a certain five-year-old boy—or the way he'd look if he had long hair.

Julie's baby sister—who had no name in the story—was a pest. She got into Julie's bottom drawer and pulled out all her sweaters. Elaina sketched Betsy with a sweater pulled half over her head, one eye and one ear sticking out, her downy hair on end, her belled boots planted heel to heel on the floor and her fat knees bent.

Julie's baby sister chewed on the cat's tail, and Elaina drew Betsy gnawing on Harrison's tail. Harrison looked pained but patient.

She drew Betsy gleefully squeezing ketchup out of the bottle that Julie had carelessly left on a kitchen chair, and drew Betsy tearing up Julie's best picture from kindergarten, the one she'd been saving to give to her grandma. She drew Betsy in a dozen different poses, then a dozen more, her pencil flying. At last she realized it was dark beyond the circle of light cast by her two drawing lamps and that her back hurt and she was hungry.

But still she worked. There was one sketch left to do. She didn't want to do it, but if she didn't do it now, she wondered if she ever would.

She drew Julie first. That was easiest. Then she drew the crib. Her pencil only hinted at the lumped shape under the blankets, rump high, one hand clutching the corner of a cloth book. It was the daddy that stopped her. The daddy that the author said was sitting on the rocking chair beside the crib with Julie and a story book on his lap.

She sketched in a shape. An elegant profile. A strong neck. A pair of firm lips and eyes that laughed. She drew powerful shoulders, neat-fingered hands, cut off jeans with ragged ends, long, bare legs, and slender feet with straight toes.

Did a father dress like that when he was reading bedtime stories? She didn't know. Her father had never read her one. She crumpled the drawing and threw it onto the floor. She started again.

When she looked up finally, it was daylight and the floor was covered with crumpled papers. Her fingers ached, but she had done it. She had gotten it right. She didn't know if the publisher would accept it. She didn't know if the author would like it, but it was done, and she knew that nothing could make her undo it. It was right.

She stretched and yawned, and the doorbell rang.

With her heart in her throat, her palms wet, and her mouth dry, she went to answer it.

She hadn't heard his van. She hadn't heard the gate slam. He read the question in her eyes.

"I was sitting on the patio," he said. "I fell asleep on the lounge. You worked all night? You look awful."

"You don't look so great yourself."

"Can I come in?"

She shook her head.

"Lainie . . ." She took a step back. Brad took one forward and then he was inside with her. He shut the door. "Why did you leave Betsy's crib outside like that? As if you couldn't wait to get rid of her stuff—and me?"

"It seemed . . . better. Easier. Not to have to force you to say . . ."

"Good-bye?"

She nodded.

He leaned back on the door and closed his eyes. "It wasn't easier! God, Lainie, it was so hard, finding it sitting there, and for you not to answer the door when I rang." He looked down at her, bleakly, wearily. If he had truly slept on the lounge chair, it hadn't been for long. "Don't you see? There has to be a definite ending to things like this. They can't be left hanging."

"Okay," she whispered. "Then do it. Say it. End it."

"Lainie . . . Could I hold you, please? Just for a minute?"

"Brad, don't do this to me! Just go. Please, go."

"I—I need to be with you for a little while. I need to hold you." His face was gray with more than fatigue. His eyes were sunken and his mouth was drawn taut. Someone he had worked over long and hard had died.

She took the one step necessary and held him tightly, feeling him tremble in her arms. Caressing the back of his head, she murmured soft phrases that had no real meaning, yet gave comfort.

Finally, he lifted his head and looked at her, trying to smile. She slipped out of his arms and took his hand. "Want to tell me about it?" she asked, leading him into her studio. She sat beside him on the couch and felt his beeper pressing into her waist. She hated it for what it symbolized.

He talked about a mother, a father, two of their three children, and the drunk who had run them off the road.

"And a little girl, four years old, has no parents, no brothers. She's alone. I can't stand it, Lainie. I can't go back there."

But when he began to wind down, when his rage ebbed and his muscles relaxed, when he said, as always, "Lainie, I'm sorry. Why do I always do this to you?" she knew he would be fine. She knew he'd go back.

"I don't mind," she said, as she always did. And it was true. While she hated the things that happened because they were usually so unjust, she didn't get as emotionally tied up as he did. Somehow, she could detach herself from it, as he, who saw it firsthand, could not. If sharing the load with her eased it for him, then she was glad to do it.

He slipped one hand under her chin and tilted her face up to his. He kissed her softly, tenderly, with a gentle persuasion that melted her against him, and she responded with all the love and longing in her soul. He lifted her in his arms, carried her to her bedroom, and laid her on the bed. She made no protest.

Silently, urgently, desperately, they loved each other, and when it was over she didn't know whose tears were wetting their faces. Still holding him tightly, she slept. When she woke, he was gone.

He didn't come again for nearly a week. Again she let him in, held him while he suffered and recovered from trauma, then loved him until they both collapsed from exhaustion.

A pattern had been set. When he wasn't there, she worked to fill her hours and her emptiness any way she could. She waited for him, made herself available to him when he needed her. She knew it was all she could have of him, and she told herself over and over that it had to be enough. She would make it be enough.

Work was good, too, and she worked very hard. In fact, she worked more than she ever had before. She completed the commission for the series long before the due date and consequently was assigned four more. The publisher asked if she wouldn't consider moving to New York City and coming on staff. The salary and benefit package was attractive, but she looked at her patio, her cat sunning himself on the garden wall, listened to Billy and Petey, home from school and arguing next door, and wrote a letter of regret.

She was quite certain that her decision had nothing to do with the fact that she spent far more time than was good for her listening for her doorbell and rushing to answer it each time it rang. One morning it rang early and she went flying out of bed, sure it was Brad, only to find that it was a short circuit in her wiring.

"Short circuit," she murmured thoughtfully several hours later after the electrician had finally gone. He had not only repaired the wiring, but had also installed melodious chimes far more to her liking than the irritating old bell had been. "That's what my life has become. A short circuit. A bell inside me is ringing even when there's no one there to push it."

When the chimes bing-bonged two days later and she saw Brad's van through the window, she got up from her work table with a new resolve in her heart.

As usual, he reached for her, but this time she evaded him. "Brad, sit down," she said quietly.

He didn't. Looking at her warily, he asked, "What's wrong?"

She drew in a deep breath and let it out slowly. "You once said that I'd have every right to expect marriage from you. That I deserve better than . . . this and that you were sure I wouldn't make demands. And you were right. I didn't. I haven't. But I can't go on this way, either, having you come to me only when your need is so great that you can't stay away. You were right, Brad. I do deserve more than you're giving me. And I want it. I want a lot more. I have needs, too, and they're not being met.

"I'm not asking you to meet them. I know you can't. You made that clear a long time ago. So I'm telling you to leave, now, and don't come back. Because I have to be free to find someone who is capable of being what I need and giving me what I deserve."

"Elaina . . ." he whispered. "Oh, Lainie. Please . . ." He swallowed and shook his head. "No. You're right."

He turned and walked away from her, out the door, and she didn't look to see if he used the steps off the porch. A long while later, she closed the door and went back to work. But this time, she wasn't sure if work was going to be enough.

Joining a fitness club helped. So did the course she took at the Community College. She didn't know if she'd ever actually want to use a computer, but it certainly opened up a whole new line of interest for her and allowed her to meet several people. Male people. She even dated a couple of them a couple of times, and told herself that she had enjoyed it.

That was all it took, she decided. Friends. Keeping busy. Smiling even when your insides were filled with cracked ice, laughing in spite of the tears in your throat. And not thinking too much.

A month passed, and then most of another. The weather was as rainy and bleak as Elaina felt inside. She wondered over and over how Brad was coping. What did he do when bad things happened and hurt him? Did he have someone to go to? Did someone hold him? Did someone listen? Did he have a doorbell to ring at midnight, certain that it would be answered?

There were days when she hated herself for what she had done to him, nights when she yearned to call the hospital and ask to talk to him, just to reassure herself that he was all right. Surely, though, he was. He must be. If he weren't all right, he would have found a way to come to her.

Or would he? Hadn't she shut every last door in his face? She had turned him away when he needed her. Oh, God, why had she done that? she asked herself one night, lying sleepless in her bed. What kind of a friend was she? And surely, before they became lovers, they had been friends. Had she the right to deny him that part of their relationship? No! No one had the right to turn her back on a friend who needed her. What if she needed him, just as a friend? Wouldn't he be there for her? He would. She knew he would.

She listened to the rain beat against the window, waiting for morning when she could call him and ask him if he wanted to come for dinner or something. Or just to talk. Or not talk, if that was what he needed. Just to sit. She had been so wrong to send him away, she was thinking, when the chimes echoed politely through the house.

Why did she smile so hugely as she leaped out of bed? Why did she neglect to put on her warm robe as she ran to the door? Why did she forget to ask who was there? She didn't know. She didn't care. It had to be Brad, and for him to be there had to be right.

Without hesitation, she drew him inside, and they wrapped their arms around each other, rocking back and forth, his soaked clothing dampening her sheer nightgown. Finally, she was able to speak.

"What is it?" she asked, stroking his face as she stepped out of his embrace. "Tell me, Brad." She ached with wanting him, hurt with love for him. She wanted to crawl back into his arms and stay there forever, but he wasn't prepared to offer her forever. And she had just told herself that she would learn to accept less.

"I need you," he said simply.

"Yes." Her voice was soft, contrite. "I know you do, Brad. Funny, isn't it? I was just lying there in bed thinking about you, thinking how wrong I was in what I did to you, sending you away like that. In the time I knew you, you became my best friend, and what I did to you was a terrible thing to do to a friend. I'm sorry, Brad. I won't send you away again. Any time you need someone to talk to, I'll try to be here for you."

"That's good," he said. "That's one of the things I'll expect in my wife."

She went very still, her hands clenched tightly in front of her. She shook her head. "You don't have to marry me. I've already said that whenever you need someone to talk to, a friend, I'll be here for you. Whenever I can, that is. I will date other men—"

She swept right on past his muttered "Like hell you will!"

"I'll continue to take classes. I won't sit and wait for you like I did before, but I won't send you away if you need me and I'm free and—"

"Elaina?"

"Yes?"

"Shut up."

"Oh."

After he had finished kissing her—for the moment—he said, "I love you. And I only want to ask you one more thing: Will you marry me? The answer, in case you might have trouble coming up with it, is yes."

She stared at him, feeling the heavy pounding of his heart against her breast.

"That's the only answer possible?"

He nodded solemnly.

With a slow, sweet smile, she nodded back. "Yes."

He lifted her in his arms and carried her to bed.

Much later, sitting up in bed and sipping hot tea, they talked.

"I should have realized it right away," he said, sliding a strand of her fine, soft hair across his lips. He breathed in the sweet scent of it, loving its texture. Then he took her cup from her and set it down by the teapot, and drew her into his arms.

"The job was getting to me badly before I met you. You made it possible for me to handle it. You helped me, somehow, to absorb the bad parts. Then, later, when you told me I couldn't come back, it started to build up so bad that I was about to quit. I started doing some heavy thinking, and I knew that it wasn't only on the bad days that I wanted you, needed to be with you. I needed—need—you on the good days too. But I was still afraid to think it could be forever."

"And now?"

"Lainie, do you think you can stand a lifetime of listening to me grouse about the lousy deal so many innocent people get in life? Is it fair of me to dump it on you when I can't carry it all by myself?"

She cradled his face against her hand. "I don't know. Is it fair that I ask you to be my strength? Is it all right for me to want you to prop me up when I can't stand alone? And I can't, Brad. These last couple of months have proven that to me. I'm not the loner I thought I was. I need you at least as much as you need me."

He kissed her palm and turned his face to look down into her eyes. "When you told me to get lost, you said that you had needs that weren't being met. I know you have a hard time talking about what you need and want, Lainie, but can you trust me enough to tell me? I want to give you everything you yearn for."

She smiled. "You're right. It isn't easy for me to talk about some things, but I can tell you a secret about me: When I want something, I fantasize it. And when I fantasize it, I draw it. When I draw it, I'll show you. Like this."

She leaned over him, opened the drawer in her bedside table, and pulled out a portfolio of finished drawings, all soft pastels, copies of the ones for *Julie's Baby Sister*.

Sitting up against the headboard, he leafed through them, swallowing the lump in his throat as he recognized Betsy in every one of them—except the last. In that one, the rump-high baby had its face hidden. The older child had her face buried against her father, asleep. But it was the parents, smiling at each other, he in the rocking chair with a story book in his hand, she in the doorway with her finger on the light switch, that made Brad's eyes glitter as he smiled at Elaina.

"Oh, sweetheart. That's us!"

"My wildest fantasy. My dearest dream," she said.

He set the pages carefully on the floor and gathered her into his arms. "Let's see what we can do about fulfilling that fantasy, love, because Lainie . . . oh, my Lainie, I want it too!"

"Forever?" she asked.

"Forever," he told her fervently. "And then some."

THE EDITOR'S CORNER

A critic once wrote that LOVESWEPT books have "the most off-the-wall titles" of any romance line. And recently, I got a letter from a reader asking me who is responsible for the "unusual titles" of our books. (Our fans are so polite; I'll bet she wanted to substitute "strange" for unusual!) Whether off-the-wall or unusual—I prefer to think of them as memorable—our titles are dreamed up by authors as well as editors. (We editors must take the responsibility for the most outrageous titles, though.) Next month you can look forward to six wonderful LOVESWEPTs that are as original, strong, amusing—yes, even as off-the-wall—as their titles.

First, **McKNIGHT IN SHINING ARMOR,** LOVESWEPT #276, by Tami Hoag, is an utterly heartwarming story of a young divorced woman, Kelsie Connors, who has two children to raise while holding down two *very* unusual jobs. She's trying to be the complete Superwoman when she meets hero Alec McKnight. Their first encounter, while hilarious, holds the potential for disaster . . . as black lace lingerie flies through the air of the conservative advertising executive's office. But Alec is enchanted, not enraged—and then Kelsie has to wonder if the "disaster" isn't what he's done to her heart. A joyous reading experience.

SHOWDOWN AT LIZARD ROCK, LOVESWEPT #277, by Sandra Chastain, features one of the most gorgeous and exciting pairs of lovers ever. Kaylyn Smith has the body of Wonder Woman and the face of Helen of Troy, and handsome hunk King Vandergriff realizes the

(continued)

moment he sets eyes on her that he's met his match. She is standing on top of Lizard Rock, protesting his construction company's building of a private club on the town's landmark. King just climbs right up there and carries her down . . . but she doesn't surrender. (Well, not immediately.) You'll delight in the feisty shenanigans of this marvelous couple.

CALIFORNIA ROYALE, LOVESWEPT #278, by Deborah Smith, is one of the most heart-stoppingly beautiful of love stories. Shea Somerton is elegant and glamorous just like the resort she runs; Duke Araiza is sexy and fast just like the Thoroughbreds he raises and trains. Both have heartbreaking pain in their pasts. And each has the fire and the understanding that the other needs. But their goals put them at cross-purposes, and neither of them can bend . . . until a shadow from Shea's early days falls over their lives. A thrilling romance.

Get out the box of tissues when you settle down to enjoy **WINTER'S DAUGHTER,** LOVESWEPT #279, by Kathleen Creighton, because you're bound to get a good laugh and a good cry from this marvelous love story. Tannis Winter, disguised as a bag-lady, has gone out onto the streets to learn about the plight of the homeless and to search for cures for their ills. But so has town councilman Dillon James, a "derelict" with mysterious attractions for the unknowing Tannis. Dillon is instantly bewitched by her courage and compassion . . . by the scent of summer on her skin and the brilliance of winter in her eyes. Their hunger for each other grows quickly . . . and to ravenous proportions. Only a risky confrontation can clear up the misunderstandings they face, so that they can finally have it all. We think you're going to treasure this very rich and very dramatic love story.

Completing the celebration of her fifth year as a published writer, the originator of continuing character romances, Iris Johansen, gives us the breathlessly emotional love story of the Sheik you met this month, exciting Damon El Karim, in **STRONG, HOT WINDS,** LOVESWEPT #280. Damon has vowed to punish the lovely Cory Brandel, the mother of his son, whom she's kept secret from him. To do so, he has her kidnapped with the

(continued)

boy and brought to Kasmara. But in his desert palace, as they set each other off, his sense of barbaric justice and her fury at his betrayal quickly turn into quite different emotions. Bewildered by the tenderness and the wild need he feels for her, Damon fears he can never have Cory's love. But at last, Cory has begun to understand what makes this complex and charismatic man tick—and she fears she isn't strong enough to give him the enduring love he so much deserves! Crème de la crème from Iris Johansen. I'm sure you join all of us at Bantam in wishing her not five, but *fifty* more years of creating great love stories!

Closing out the month in a very big way is **PARADISE CAFE,** LOVESWEPT #281, by Adrienne Staff. And what a magnificent tale this is. Beautiful Abby Clarke is rescued by ruggedly handsome outdoorsman Jack Gallagher—a man of few words and fast moves, especially when trying to haul in the lady whom destiny has put in his path. But Abby is not a risk taker. She's an earnest, hardworking young woman who's always put her family first . . . but Jack is an impossible man to walk away from with his sweet, wild passion that makes her yearn to forget about being safe. And Jack is definitely *not* safe for Abby . . . he's a man with wandering feet. You'll relish the way the stay-at-home and the vagabond find that each has a home in the center of the other's heart. A true delight.

I trust that you'll agree with me that the six LOVESWEPTs next month are as memorable as their off-the-wall titles!

Enjoy!

Carolyn Nichols

Carolyn Nichols
Editor
LOVESWEPT
Bantam Books
666 Fifth Avenue
New York, NY 10103

THE HOMETOWN HUNK CONTEST

FOR EVERY WOMAN WHO HAS EVER SAID—
"I know a man who looks
just like the hero of this book"
—HAVE WE GOT A CONTEST FOR YOU!

To help celebrate our fifth year of publishing LOVESWEPT we are having a fabulous, fun-filled event called THE HOMETOWN HUNK contest. We are going to reissue six classic early titles by six of your favorite authors.

***DARLING OBSTACLES* by Barbara Boswell**
***IN A CLASS BY ITSELF* by Sandra Brown**
***C.J.'S FATE* by Kay Hooper**
***THE LADY AND THE UNICORN* by Iris Johansen**
***CHARADE* by Joan Elliott Pickart**
***FOR THE LOVE OF SAMI* by Fayrene Preston**

Here, as in the backs of all July, August, and September 1988 LOVESWEPTS you will find "cover notes" just like the ones we prepare at Bantam as the background for our art director to create our covers. These notes will describe the hero and heroine, give a teaser on the plot, and suggest a scene for the cover. Your part in the contest will be to see if a great looking local man—or men, if your hometown is so blessed—fits our description of one of the heroes of the six books we will reissue.

THE HOMETOWN HUNK who is selected (one for each of the six titles) will be flown to New York via United Airlines and will stay at the Loews Summit Hotel—the ideal hotel for business or pleasure in midtown Manhattan—for two nights. All travel arrangements made by Reliable Travel International, Incorporated. He will be the model for the new cover of the book which will be released in mid-1989. The six people who send in the winning photos of their HOMETOWN HUNK will receive a pre-selected assortment of LOVESWEPT books free for one year. Please see the Official Rules above the Official Entry Form for full details and restrictions.

We can't wait to start judging those pictures! Oh, and you must let the man you've chosen know that you're entering him in the contest. After all, if he wins he'll have to come to New York.

Have fun. Here's your chance to get the cover-lover of your dreams!

Carolyn Nichols

Carolyn Nichols
Editor
LOVESWEPT
Bantam Books
666 Fifth Avenue
New York, NY 10102–0023

THE HOMETOWN HUNK CONTEST

DARLING OBSTACLES

(Originally Published as LOVESWEPT #95)

By Barbara Boswell

COVER NOTES

The Characters:

Hero:
GREG WILDER's gorgeous body and "to-die-for" good looks haven't hurt him in the dating department, but when most women discover he's a widower with four kids, they head for the hills! Greg has the hard, muscular build of an athlete, and his light brown hair, which he wears neatly parted on the side, is streaked blond by the sun. Add to that his aquamarine blue eyes that sparkle when he laughs, and his sensual mouth and generous lower lip, and you're probably wondering what woman in her right mind wouldn't want Greg's strong, capable surgeon's hands working their magic on her—kids or no kids!

Personality Traits:
An acclaimed neurosurgeon, Greg Wilder is a celebrity of sorts in the planned community of Woodland, Maryland. Authoritative, debonair, self-confident, his reputation for engaging in one casual relationship after another almost overshadows his prowess as a doctor. In reality, Greg dates more out of necessity than anything else, since he has to attend one social function after another. He considers most of the events boring and wishes he could spend more time with his children. But his profession is a difficult and demanding one—and being both father and mother to four kids isn't any less so. A thoughtful, generous, sometimes befuddled father, Greg tries to do it all. Cerebral, he uses his intellect and skill rather than physical strength to win his victories. However, he never expected to come up against one Mary Magdalene May!

Heroine:
MARY MAGDALENE MAY, called Maggie by her friends, is the thirty-two-year-old mother of three children. She has shoulder-length auburn hair, and green eyes that shout her Irish heritage. With high cheekbones and an upturned nose covered with a smattering of freckles, Maggie thinks of herself more as the girl-next-door type. Certainly, she believes, she could never be one of Greg Wilder's beautiful escorts.

Setting: The small town of Woodland, Maryland

The Story:
Surgeon Greg Wilder wanted to court the feisty and beautiful widow who'd been caring for his four kids, but she just wouldn't let him past her doorstep! Sure that his interest was only casual, and that he preferred more sophisticated women, Maggie May vowed to keep Greg at arm's length. But he wouldn't take no for an answer. And once he'd crashed through her defenses and pulled her into his arms, he was tireless—and reckless—in his campaign to win her over. Maggie had found it tough enough to resist one determined doctor; now he threatened to call in his kids and hers as reinforcements—seven rowdy snags to romance!

Cover scene:
As if romancing Maggie weren't hard enough, Greg can't seem to find time to spend with her without their children around. Stealing a private moment on the stairs in Maggie's house, Greg and Maggie embrace. She is standing one step above him, but she still has to look up at him to see into his eyes. Greg's hands are on her hips, and her hands are resting on his shoulders. Maggie is wearing a very sheer, short pink nightgown, and Greg has on wheat-colored jeans and a navy and yellow striped rugby shirt. Do they have time to kiss?

THE HOMETOWN HUNK CONTEST

IN A CLASS BY ITSELF

(Originally Published as LOVESWEPT #66)

By Sandra Brown

COVER NOTES

The Characters:

Hero:
LOGAN WEBSTER would have no trouble posing for a Scandinavian travel poster. His wheat-colored hair always seems to be tousled, defying attempts to control it, and falls across his wide forehead. Thick eyebrows one shade darker than his hair accentuate his crystal blue eyes. He has a slender nose that flairs slightly over a mouth that testifies to both sensitivity and strength. The faint lines around his eyes and alongside his mouth give the impression that reaching the ripe age of 30 wasn't all fun and games for him. Logan's square, determined jaw is punctuated by a vertical cleft. His broad shoulders and narrow waist add to his tall, lean appearance.

Personality traits:
Logan Webster has had to scrape and save and fight for everything he's gotten. Born into a poor farm family, he was driven to succeed and overcome his "wrong side of the tracks" image. His businesses include cattle, real estate, and natural gas. Now a pillar of the community, Logan's life has been a true rags-to-riches story. Only Sandra Brown's own words can describe why he is masculinity epitomized: "Logan had 'the walk,' that saddle-tramp saunter that was inherent to native Texan men, passed down through generations of cowboys. It was, without even trying to be, sexy. The unconscious roll of the hips, the slow strut, the flexed knees, the slouching stance, the deceptive laziness that hid a latent aggressiveness." Wow! And not only does he have "the walk," but he's fun

and generous and kind. Even with his wealth, he feels at home living in his small hometown with simple, hard-working, middle-class, backbone-of-America folks. A born leader, people automatically gravitate toward him.

Heroine:
DANI QUINN is a sophisticated twenty-eight-year-old woman. Dainty, her body compact, she is utterly feminine. Dani's pale, lustrous hair is moonlight and honey spun together, and because it is very straight, she usually wears it in a chignon. With golden eyes to match her golden hair, Dani is the one woman Logan hasn't been able to get off his mind for the ten years they've been apart.

Setting: Primarily on Logan's ranch in East Texas.

The Story:
Ten years had passed since Dani Quinn had graduated from high school in the small Texas town, ten years since the night her elopement with Logan Webster had ended in disaster. Now Dani approached her tenth reunion with uncertainty. Logan would be there . . . Logan, the only man who'd ever made her shiver with desire and need, but would she have the courage to face the fury in his eyes? She couldn't defend herself against his anger and hurt—to do so would demand she reveal the secret sorrow she shared with no one. Logan's touch had made her his so long ago. Could he reach past the pain to make her his for all time?

Cover Scene:
It's sunset, and Logan and Dani are standing beside the swimming pool on his ranch, embracing. The pool is surrounded by semitropical plants and lush flower beds. In the distance, acres of rolling pasture land resembling a green lake undulate into dense, piney woods. Dani is wearing a strapless, peacock blue bikini and sandals with leather ties that wrap around her ankles. Her hair is straight and loose, falling to the middle of her back. Logan has on a light-colored pair of corduroy shorts and a short-sleeved designer knit shirt in a pale shade of yellow.

THE HOMETOWN HUNK CONTEST

C.J.'S FATE

(Originally Published as LOVESWEPT #32)

By Kay Hooper

COVER NOTES

The Characters:

Hero:
FATE WESTON easily could have walked straight off an Indian reservation. His raven black hair and strong, well-molded features testify to his heritage. But somewhere along the line genetics threw Fate a curve—his eyes are the deepest, darkest blue imaginable! Above those blue eyes are dark slanted eyebrows, and fanning out from those eyes are faint laugh lines—the only sign of the fact that he's thirty-four years old. Tall, Fate moves with easy, loose-limbed grace. Although he isn't an athlete, Fate takes very good care of himself, and it shows in his strong physique. Striking at first glance and fascinating with each succeeding glance, the serious expressions on his face make him look older than his years, but with one smile he looks boyish again.

Personality traits:
Fate possesses a keen sense of humor. His heavy-lidded, intelligent eyes are capable of concealment, but there is a shrewdness in them that reveals the man hadn't needed college or a law degree to be considered intelligent. The set of his head tells you that he is proud—perhaps even a bit arrogant. He is attractive and perfectly well aware of that fact. Unconventional, paradoxical, tender, silly, lusty, gentle, comical, serious, absurd, and endearing are all words that come to mind when you think of Fate. He is not ashamed to be everything a man can be. A defense attorney by profession, one can detect a bit of frustrated actor in his character. More than anything else, though, it's the

impression of humor about him—reinforced by the elusive dimple in his cheek—that makes Fate Weston a scrumptious hero!

Heroine:
C.J. ADAMS is a twenty-six-year-old research librarian. Unaware of her own attractiveness, C.J. tends to play down her pixylike figure and tawny gold eyes. But once she meets Fate, she no longer feels that her short, burnished copper curls and the sprinkling of freckles on her nose make her unappealing. He brings out the vixen in her, and changes the smart, bookish woman who professed to have no interest in men into the beautiful, sexy woman she really was all along. Now, if only he could get her to tell him what C.J. stands for!

Setting: Ski lodge in Aspen, Colorado

The Story:
C.J. Adams had been teased enough about her seeming lack of interest in the opposite sex. On a ski trip with her five best friends, she impulsively embraced a handsome stranger, pretending they were secret lovers—and the delighted lawyer who joined in her impetuous charade seized the moment to deepen the kiss. Astonished at his reaction, C.J. tried to nip their romance in the bud—but found herself nipping at his neck instead! She had met her match in a man who could answer her witty remarks with clever ripostes of his own, and a lover whose caresses aroused in her a passionate need she'd never suspected that she could feel. Had destiny somehow tossed them together?

Cover Scene:
C.J. and Fate virtually have the ski slopes to themselves early one morning, and they take advantage of it! Frolicking in a snow drift, Fate is covering C.J. with snow—and kisses! They are flushed from the cold weather and from the excitement of being in love. C.J. is wearing a sky-blue, one-piece, tight-fitting ski outfit that zips down the front. Fate is wearing a navy blue parka and matching ski pants.

THE HOMETOWN HUNK CONTEST

THE LADY AND THE UNICORN

(Originally Published as LOVESWEPT #29)

By Iris Johansen

COVER NOTES

The Characters:

Hero:
Not classically handsome, RAFE SANTINE's blunt, craggy features reinforce the quality of overpowering virility about him. He has wide, Slavic cheekbones and a bold, thrusting chin, which give the impression of strength and authority. Thick black eyebrows are set over piercing dark eyes. He wears his heavy, dark hair long. His large frame measures in at almost six feet four inches, and it's hard to believe that a man with such brawny shoulders and strong thighs could exhibit the pantherlike grace which characterizes Rafe's movements. Rafe Santine is definitely a man to be reckoned with, and heroine Janna Cannon does just that!

Personality traits:
Our hero is a man who radiates an aura of power and danger, and women find him intriguing and irresistible. Rafe Santine is a self-made billionaire at the age of thirty-eight. Almost entirely self-educated, he left school at sixteen to work on his first construction job, and by the time he was twenty-three, he owned the company. From there he branched out into real estate, computers, and oil. Rafe reportedly changes mistresses as often as he changes shirts. His reputation for ruthless brilliance has been earned over years of fighting to the top of the economic ladder from the slums of New York. His gruff manner and hard personality hide the tender, vulnerable side of him. Rafe also possesses an insatiable thirst for knowledge that is a passion with him. Oddly enough, he has a wry sense of

humor that surfaces unexpectedly from time to time. And, though cynical to the extreme, he never lets his natural skepticism interfere with his innate sense of justice.

Heroine:
JANNA CANNON, a game warden for a small wildlife preserve, is a very dedicated lady. She is tall at five feet nine inches and carries herself in a stately way. Her long hair is dark brown and is usually twisted into a single thick braid in back. Of course, Rafe never lets her keep her hair braided when they make love! Janna is one quarter Cherokee Indian by heritage, and she possesses the dark eyes and skin of her ancestors.

Setting: Rafe's estate in Carmel, California

The Story:
Janna Cannon scaled the high walls of Rafe Santine's private estate, afraid of nothing and determined to appeal to the powerful man who could save her beloved animal preserve. She bewitched his guard dogs, then cast a spell of enchantment over him as well. Janna's profound grace, her caring nature, made the tough and proud Rafe grow mercurial in her presence. She offered him a gift he'd never risked reaching out for before—but could he trust his own emotions enough to open himself to her love?

Cover Scene:
In the gazebo overlooking the rugged cliffs at the edge of the Pacific Ocean, Rafe and Janna share a passionate moment together. The gazebo is made of redwood and the interior is small and cozy. Scarlet cushions cover the benches, and matching scarlet curtains hang from the eaves, caught back by tasseled sashes to permit the sea breeze to whip through the enclosure. Rafe is wearing black suede pants and a charcoal gray crew-neck sweater. Janna is wearing a safari-style khaki shirt-and-slacks outfit and suede desert boots. They embrace against the breathtaking backdrop of wild, crashing, white-crested waves pounding the rocks and cliffs below.

THE HOMETOWN HUNK CONTEST

CHARADE

(Originally Published as LOVESWEPT #74)

By Joan Elliott Pickart

COVER NOTES

The Characters:

Hero:
The phrase tall, dark, and handsome was coined to describe TENNES WHITNEY. His coal black hair reaches past his collar in back, and his fathomless steel gray eyes are framed by the kind of thick, dark lashes that a woman would kill to have. Darkly tanned, Tennes has a straight nose and a square chin, with—you guessed it!—a Kirk Douglas cleft. Tennes oozes masculinity and virility. He's a handsome son-of-a-gun!

Personality traits:
A shrewd, ruthless business tycoon, Tennes is a man of strength and principle. He's perfected the art of buying floundering companies and turning them around financially, then selling them at a profit. He possesses a sixth sense about business—in short, he's a winner! But there are two sides to his personality. Always in cool command, Tennes, who fears no man or challenge, is rendered emotionally vulnerable when faced with his elderly aunt's illness. His deep devotion to the woman who raised him clearly casts him as a warm, compassionate guy—nct at all like the tough-as-nails executive image he presents. Leave it to heroine Whitney Jordan to discover the real man behind the complicated enigma.

Heroine:
WHITNEY JORDAN's russet-colored hair floats past her shoulders in glorious waves. Her emerald green eyes, full breasts, and long, slender legs—not to mention her peaches-

and-cream complexion—make her eye-poppingly attrac
tive. How can Tennes resist the twenty-six-year-old beauty
And how can Whitney consider becoming serious wit
him? If their romance flourishes, she may end up bein
Whitney Whitney!

Setting: Los Angeles, California

The Story:
One moment writer Whitney Jordan was strolling the aisle
of McNeil's Department Store, plotting the untimely de
mise of a soap opera heartthrob; the next, she was near
knocked over by a real-life stunner who implored her to b
his fiancée! The ailing little gray-haired aunt who'd raise
him had one final wish, he said—to see her dear nephe
Tennes married to the wonderful girl he'd described in hi
letters . . . only that girl hadn't existed—until now! Ter
nes promised the masquerade would last only throug
lunch, but Whitney gave such an inspired performanc
that Aunt Olive refused to let her go. And what began as
playful romantic deception grew more breathlessly real b
the minute. . . .

Cover Scene:
Whitney's living room is bright and cheerful. The gra
carpeting and blue sofa with green and blue throw pi
lows gives the apartment a cool but welcoming appea
ance. Sitting on the sofa next to Tennes, Whitney is wearin
a black crepe dress that is simply cut but stunning. It
cut low over her breasts and held at the shoulders by thi
straps. The skirt falls to her knees in soft folds and th
bodice is nipped in at the waist with a matching belt. Sh
has on black high heels, but prefers not to wear ar
jewelry to spoil the simplicity of the dress. Tennes is dresse
in a black suit with a white silk shirt and a deep red tie

THE HOMETOWN HUNK CONTEST

FOR THE LOVE OF SAMI

(Originally Published as LOVESWEPT #34)

By Fayrene Preston

COVER NOTES

Hero:
DANIEL PARKER-ST. JAMES is every woman's dream come true. With glossy black hair and warm, reassuring blue eyes, he makes our heroine melt with just a glance. Daniel's lean face is chiseled into assertive planes. His lips are full and firmly sculptured, and his chin has the determined and arrogant thrust to it only a man who's sure of himself can carry off. Daniel has a lot in common with Clark Kent. Both wear glasses, and when Daniel removes them to make love to Sami, she thinks he really is Superman!

Personality traits:
Daniel Parker-St. James is one of the Twin Cities' most respected attorneys. He's always in the news, either in the society columns with his latest society lady, or on the front page with his headline cases. He's brilliant and takes on only the toughest cases—usually those that involve millions of dollars. Daniel has a reputation for being a deadly opponent in the courtroom. Because he's from a socially prominent family and is a Harvard graduate, it's expected that he'll run for the Senate one day. Distinguished-looking and always distinctively dressed—he's fastidious about his appearance—Daniel gives off an unassailable air of authority and absolute control.

Heroine:
SAMUELINA (SAMI) ADKINSON is secretly a wealthy heiress. No one would guess. She lives in a converted warehouse loft, dresses to suit no one but herself, and dabbles in the creative arts. Sami is twenty-six years old, with

long, honey-colored hair. She wears soft, wispy bangs and has very thick brown lashes framing her golden eyes. Of medium height, Sami has to look up to gaze into Daniel's deep blue eyes.

Setting: St. Paul, Minnesota

The Story:
Unpredictable heiress Sami Adkinson had endeared herself to the most surprising people—from the bag ladies in the park she protected . . . to the mobster who appointed himself her guardian . . . to her exasperated but loving friends. Then Sami was arrested while demonstrating to save baby seals, and it took powerful attorney Daniel Parker-St. James to bail her out. Daniel was smitten, soon cherishing Sami and protecting her from her night fears. Sami reveled in his love—and resisted it too. And holding on to Sami, Daniel discovered, was like trying to hug quicksilver. . . .

Cover Scene:
The interior of Daniel's house is very grand and supremely formal, the decor sophisticated, refined, and quietly tasteful, just like Daniel himself. Rich traditional fabrics cover plush oversized custom sofas and Regency wing chairs. Queen Anne furniture is mixed with Chippendale and is subtly complemented with Oriental accent pieces. In the library, floor-to-ceiling bookcases filled with rare books provide the backdrop for Sami and Daniel's embrace. Sami is wearing a gold satin sheath gown. The dress has a high neckline, but in back is cut provocatively to the waist. Her jewels are exquisite. The necklace is made up of clusters of flowers created by large, flawless diamonds. From every cluster a huge, perfectly matched teardrop emerald hangs. The earrings are composed of an even larger flower cluster, and an equally huge teardrop-shaped emerald hangs from each one. Daniel is wearing a classic, elegant tuxedo.

LOVESWEPT® HOMETOWN HUNK CONTEST

OFFICIAL RULES

IN A CLASS BY ITSELF by Sandra Brown
FOR THE LOVE OF SAMI by Fayrene Preston
C.J.'S FATE by Kay Hooper
THE LADY AND THE UNICORN by Iris Johansen
CHARADE by Joan Elliott Pickart
DARLING OBSTACLES by Barbara Boswell

1. NO PURCHASE NECESSARY. Enter the HOMETOWN HUNK contest by completing the Official Entry Form below and enclosing a sharp color full-length photograph (easy to see details, with the photo being no smaller than 2½" × 3½") of the man you think perfectly represents one of the heroes from the above-listed books which are described in the accompanying Loveswept cover notes. Please be sure to fill out the Official Entry Form completely, and also be sure to clearly print on the back of the man's photograph the man's name, address, city, state, zip code, telephone number, date of birth, your name, address, city, state, zip code, telephone number, your relationship, if any, to the man (e.g. wife, girlfriend) as well as the title of the Loveswept book for which you are entering the man. If you do not have an Official Entry Form, you can print all of the required information on a 3" × 5" card and attach it to the photograph with all the necessary information printed on the back of the photograph as well. YOUR HERO MUST SIGN BOTH THE BACK OF THE OFFICIAL ENTRY FORM (OR 3" × 5" CARD) AND THE PHOTOGRAPH TO SIGNIFY HIS CONSENT TO BEING ENTERED IN THE CONTEST. Completed entries should be sent to:

BANTAM BOOKS
HOMETOWN HUNK CONTEST
Department CN
666 Fifth Avenue
New York, New York 10102–0023

All photographs and entries become the property of Bantam Books and will not be returned under any circumstances.

2. Six men will be chosen by the Loveswept authors as a HOMETOWN HUNK (one HUNK per Loveswept title). By entering the contest, each winner and each person who enters a winner agrees to abide by Bantam Books' rules and to be subject to Bantam Books' eligibility requirements. Each winning HUNK and each person who enters a winner will be required to sign all papers deemed necessary by Bantam Books before receiving any prize. Each winning HUNK will be flown via **United Airlines** from his closest United Airlines-serviced city to New York City and will stay at the Summit Hotel—the ideal hotel for business or pleasure in midtown Manhattan—for two nights. Winning HUNKS' meals and hotel transfers will be provided by Bantam Books. Travel and hotel arrangements are made by Reliable Travel International, Inc. and are subject to availability and to Bantam Books' date requirements. Each winning HUNK will pose with a female model at a photographer's studio for a photograph that will serve as the basis of a Loveswept front cover. Each winning HUNK will receive a $150.00 modeling fee. Each winning HUNK will be required to sign an Affidavit of Eligibility and Model's Release supplied by Bantam Books. (Approximate retail value of HOMETOWN HUNK'S PRIZE: $900.00). The six people who send in a winning HOMETOWN HUNK photograph that is used by Bantam will receive free for one year each, LOVESWEPT romance paperback books published by Bantam during that year. (Approximate retail value: $180.00.) Each person who submits a winning photograph

will also be required to sign an Affidavit of Eligibility and Promotional Release supplied by Bantam Books. All winning HUNKS' (as well as the people who submit the winning photographs) names, addresses, biographical data and likenesses may be used by Bantam Books for publicity and promotional purposes without any additional compensation. There will be no prize substitutions or cash equivalents made.

3. All completed entries must be received by Bantam Books no later than September 15, 1988. Bantam Books is not responsible for lost or misdirected entries. The finalists will be selected by Loveswept editors and the six winning HOMETOWN HUNKS will be selected by the six authors of the participating Loveswept books. Winners will be selected on the basis of how closely the judges believe they reflect the descriptions of the books' heroes. Winners will be notified on or about October 31, 1988. If there are insufficient entries or if in the judges' opinions, no entry is suitable or adequately reflects the descriptions of the hero(s) in the book(s), Bantam may decide not to award a prize for the applicable book(s) and may reissue the book(s) at its discretion.

4. The contest is open to residents of the U.S. and Canada, except the Province of Quebec, and is void where prohibited by law. All federal and local regulations apply. Employees of Reliable Travel International, Inc., United Airlines, the Summit Hotel, and the Bantam Doubleday Dell Publishing Group, Inc., their subsidiaries and affiliates, and their immediate families are ineligible to enter.

5. For an extra copy of the Official Rules, the Official Entry Form, and the accompanying Loveswept cover notes, send your request and a self-addressed stamped envelope (Vermont and Washington State residents need not affix postage) before August 20, 1988 to the address listed in Paragraph 1 above.

LOVESWEPT® HOMETOWN HUNK OFFICIAL ENTRY FORM

BANTAM BOOKS
HOMETOWN HUNK CONTEST
Dept. CN
666 Fifth Avenue
New York, New York 10102–0023

HOMETOWN HUNK CONTEST

YOUR NAME______________________________

YOUR ADDRESS______________________________

CITY________________STATE____________ZIP________

THE NAME OF THE LOVESWEPT BOOK FOR WHICH YOU ARE ENTERING THIS PHOTO

____________________by____________________

YOUR RELATIONSHIP TO YOUR HERO____________________

YOUR HERO'S NAME______________________________

YOUR HERO'S ADDRESS____________________________

CITY________________STATE____________ZIP________

YOUR HERO'S TELEPHONE #________________________

YOUR HERO'S DATE OF BIRTH________________________

YOUR HERO'S SIGNATURE CONSENTING TO HIS PHOTOGRAPH ENTRY

____